INNER CIRCLE

INNER CIRCLE
A PRIVATE NOVEL

KATE BRIAN

SIMON AND SCHUSTER

First published in Great Britain in 2008 by Simon and Schuster UK Ltd
A CBS COMPANY
This edition published 2009

Originally published in the USA in 2007 by Simon Pulse,
an imprint of Simon & Schuster Children's Division, New York.

ALLOYENTERTAINMENT   Produced by Alloy Entertainment
151 West 26th Street, New York, NY 10001

Simon & Schuster UK Ltd
1st Floor, 222 Gray's Inn Road, London WC1X 8HB

This book is a work of fiction. Names, characters, places and incidents are either
the product of the author's imagination or are used fictitiously. Any resemblance
to actual people living or dead, events or locales is entirely coincidental.

A CIP catalogue record for this book is available from the British Library.

ISBN 978-1-84738-218-4

1 3 5 7 9 10 8 6 4 2

Printed by CPI Cox & Wyman, Reading, Berkshire RG1 8EX

www.simonandschuster.co.uk

NEW YEAR

An early morning rain had come and gone, leaving behind a wet sheen that shimmered on the trees alongside the road. Weightless clouds chased the breeze across the bright blue sky. The sun made everything sparkle. There were crumpled, grease-stained fast food wrappers at my feet, and the stale smell of coffee clung to the car, but outside the world looked new. Clean. Hopeful. Even the sign welcoming students to campus had been freshened. Not replaced, of course, but the branches that used to obscure it had been trimmed back. The weeds and wildflowers tamed. It was a new year. A new start.

My father drove under the gates and started the long wind up the hill toward campus. I held my breath until the stone spire atop the Easton Academy chapel rose up from the trees. My pulse, already racing, started to sprint. I leaned forward between the two front seats, to gauge my mother's reaction. She stared out the passenger-side window of our dusty, dented Subaru, slack jawed.

"The catalog does not do this place justice," she said.

"What did I tell you?" my father replied with a hint of pride.

He, after all, had seen Easton before. My mother had not. She had always been in too much of a bitter, prescription-pill haze to join us on the long drive from Croton, Pennsylvania, to Easton, Connecticut. Or even to care that I was leaving. But that was all over now. Mom was sober. Had been since January. She'd gained weight. Had color in her face. Actually washed her hair now. Daily. I had only been home to see this behavior for two weeks, but seen it I had. With my own two eyes. Before that, I had spent most of the summer on Martha's Vineyard with Natasha and her family, waitressing at a waterside seafood restaurant and learning how to sail from Natasha and her dad. Once Natasha had left for Dartmouth, I had come home for a quick pit stop to find the house clean and freshly painted, the fridge fully stocked, my mother's bed actually made. Two weeks later I was still adjusting to the new and improved Mom.

"Reed, it's beautiful," my mother said, turning to me with a smile. Actually focusing her eyes on me. No darting. No glazing over. Focused. On me. "I still can't believe you go here."

I sighed. "Neither can I."

Especially after everything that had happened last year. In my first few months at Easton I had fallen in love for the first time, lost my virginity, made friends with the most powerful girls at school . . . and stood by totally naïve while one of them had brutally murdered my boyfriend. And that was only the beginning.

But no. I was not going to think about that. I sat back and clenched my hands into fists, digging my fingernails into my palms. I was making a new start this year. Last year was over. Last year couldn't touch me. Those people were all gone. Transferred or committed or just gone. This year could be anything I wanted it to be.

My heart fluttered with nerves and excitement as my father pulled out of the trees and onto the circle in front of the underclassmen dorms. Kiki Rosen and Diana Waters stood next to a black town car as their oversized Coach and Louis Vuitton suitcases were unloaded for them. Kiki had chopped her blond hair into a pixie cut and had dyed her bangs pink, but she still had an iPod permanently attached to her ears. Diana had grown her hair out so that it tumbled over her shoulders, and she seemed taller—older. They looked up as my car passed by and waved. I waved back and smiled. Familiar faces. Last year on this day I had known no one. Last year I had felt like I might never belong. Now there were people to welcome me. Everything really was going to be different.

My dad pulled the Subaru up in front of a sleek white Mercedes and killed the engine. I climbed out and stretched, looking up at the gleaming windows of Bradwell. I could tell from the walkway that the rooms had already been decorated and personalized. Curtains hung in several of the windows, and someone up there was listening to Avril at top volume. There had been a few changes at Easton this year. According to the information packet I'd received over the summer, there was a new headmaster, and he was already making his presence known. One of his changes was the arrival schedule. Freshmen and sophomores had already been on campus for twenty-four hours, giving them time to settle in before the upperclassmen arrived, and making the circle less packed and chaotic for unloading. My mother got out and tipped her head back, shielding her eyes with her hand as she looked up at the gray stone facade.

"This was my first dorm," I told her. "Billings House is behind it, on the quad."

Just saying the word *Billings* brought on a rush of anxiety. I had almost died there. Someone who I'd thought was my friend had actually attempted to murder me on the roof. The very person who had killed the guy I loved. Or thought I loved. I wasn't sure if I'd ever know how I'd really felt about Thomas Pearson, now that he was gone.

My fingernails dug into my palms again. Billings wasn't that place. Not anymore. Ariana was gone. This year—just like spring semester last year—the house would be full of friends. A light breeze tossed my hair back from my face. I looked up at the sun and smiled.

It was a new year. I took a deep breath, letting hope crowd out the fear.

"Well, that's everything," my father said, slapping his hands on his jeans. "These other girls sure have a lot of stuff."

I looked up and down the line of cars. There were mountains of luggage and electronics and plastic boxes and linens. My two bags, new leather backpack, and bed-in-a-bag did look sorry in comparison. I reached into the car and pulled out my laptop case. It and the computer inside it had been gifts from Natasha at the end of the summer.

A girl who wins First Honors for two straight quarters cannot be seen writing all her papers at a library computer, she'd told me. *You are not a caveperson.*

Yes, after two unstellar quarters at the beginning of the year (blame all the drama), I had come back in the spring with academic vengeance and taken Firsts in both March and June. Natasha, overachiever that she was, had been so proud. I smiled now, thinking of her. Of how much I'd miss rooming with her. My nerves sizzled with anticipation, wondering who my new roommate would be. I hoped it was someone good. Someone normal. Someone I could be friends with.

"Everything okay, kiddo?" my father asked, laying his warm hand on my shoulder.

"Everything's fine. This is going to be a good year," I told him with a confident smile. "Definitely better than last."

"Well, that shouldn't be too hard to accomplish," he joked.

My mother and I both laughed. My heart was suddenly so full, it threatened to swallow me whole. Look at us. Standing there together. We could almost be a normal family. Normal. There was a word I didn't get to use very often.

"Thanks so much, you guys," I said, hugging my father first.

"Work hard, kiddo," my dad said, kissing the top of my head.

I turned to my mother. Her eyes shone with tears. Something caught in my throat as I leaned in to hug her.

"I'm so proud of you, Reed," she said haltingly.

"Thanks, Mom," I replied.

Then they were back in the car. Starting the engine. Driving away. My mother pressed her fingertips to the window in a wave. I lifted my arm in return. Waited there until the dented Pennsylvania license plate had dipped behind the hill. At that second I realized with a start that I was going to miss my mother. Actually going to miss her.

I picked up my things and headed for Billings filled with a whole new confidence. Suddenly, anything felt possible.

PEACE

"Against my better judgment, the dean of academics granted you both your electives. The Modern Novel on top of junior English shouldn't be too challenging. But taking Advanced Placement Chemistry as well as the required Advanced Placement Biology in one year is a bit ambitious, even for you."

Mrs. Naylor's jowls had grown. They hung so low over her collar, she could have easily tucked them in. Her eyes swam in their sockets as she looked across her desk at me with a disapproving expression I had long since grown accustomed to. Behind her the wooden bookcases were jammed with dusty tomes, overflowing into haphazard piles on the floor. The rancid onion smell that always permeated her office now had a more sour tinge to it. Like something had crawled in here, eaten the rancid onions, then died.

"Well, I'm sure the dean wouldn't have allowed me to take them if he didn't think I was up to it," I replied sweetly, slipping my new schedule into my bag.

"On the contrary. Students who earn First Honors are always given their choice of courses, no matter what those of us who know better might think," she said, the jowls flapping around.

I had to press my lips together to keep from laughing. Last year she had intimidated me. This year she and her badly drawn eyeliner were just ridiculous.

"Is there anything else?" I asked.

She narrowed her eyes. Folded her craggy fingers on her desk. "No. You may go. But I trust I'll be seeing you and your drop slip very soon."

I stood up, sliding the wooden chair back with a loud scrape. "I wouldn't count on that."

I turned my back on her irritated face, feeling very Noelle Lange, and smiled to myself. Very rarely, I managed to say exactly what I wanted to say at the moment I wanted to say it, and at those moments I always thought of Noelle. As I stepped out into the sun, I wondered where she was right then. Whether she was thinking of Easton. Whether she was wishing she were here. Last year I had heard that her father's lawyers had exhibited their Olympic-level plea bargaining skills to get her kidnap charges reduced, then landed her the relatively cushy punishment of probation and community service. But I had no firsthand knowledge. I hadn't heard one word from Noelle since Christmas Day, when she'd called to convince me to come back to Easton. Not an e-mail, not a text, not a phone call. Sometimes my world felt empty without her in it. Sometimes I felt beyond lucky to be free of her.

But I knew one thing for sure: Without Noelle, I wouldn't be here. I wouldn't be alive, for one. But I wouldn't be here at Easton if she hadn't made me promise to come back. I wouldn't have all those amazing memories from last spring. Wouldn't have this hope fluttering in my chest as I strolled away from Hull Hall. If not for her, I'd be back in Croton, watching Tommy Colón make obscene hand gestures every time Principal Weiss turned his bad eye on the auditorium. High comedy, that.

"Pass it! Pass it!"

About a dozen members of the boy's varsity soccer team were scrimmaging in the center of the quad, the sleeves of their dress shirts rolled up, their shoes discarded on the sidelines in favor of cleats and sneakers. I paused. Something about this felt familiar. A déjà vu moment. I heard my name on the breeze, and my heart all but stopped.

Thomas.

I looked at the ground. This was almost the exact spot where I'd nearly tripped over him last year. Where we'd first met. First flirted. First started whatever it was we had. My scalp tightened. My fingertips tingled. He'd been here. He'd been right here. . . .

"Reed!"

I turned around and barely had time to catch my breath before Josh Hollis barreled into me at full speed. He grabbed me up in his arms, lifting me right off my feet.

"Hi!" I breathed.

I clung to him. Buried my face in that warm spot between his neck and his shoulder. He smelled exactly the same. Like evergreens and fresh paint. God, this felt good. This relief. Like coming home. Josh was my home. Not Martha's Vineyard. Not Croton, Pennsylvania. Not Easton itself. But Josh. I hadn't seen him since the last day of school in June, and while the summer had seemed to drag and drag without him, suddenly it felt as if no time had passed at all.

"God, I missed you!" he said, pulling back to plant a firm kiss on my lips.

"Me, too!" I giggled. Giggled. Reed Brennan didn't giggle. Not often, anyway.

Josh tried to put me down again, but our feet tangled up and we went over. Laughing. His face hovered over mine. His green eyes danced with happiness. His dark blond curls had been cropped close to his head in a neat, preppy cut, but one stray curl still stuck out behind his right ear, unwilling to conform.

"Hmmm." Josh looked down at me, stretched out right there in the middle of the quad. "This could be something."

My heart skipped a beat. "Could be."

He glanced around quickly, checking for authority figures. Then, coast clear, he leaned in to kiss me, really kiss me, while his teammates hooted and hollered and shouted lewd things behind us. When Josh pulled back again, he ran the tip of his finger from my temple to my chin. He was breathless.

"Next summer," he said quietly, "let's not do this apart thing."

TRADITION, HONOUR, INTIMIDATION

I smiled, utterly and completely at peace. "Yes. Let's not."

"Reed!"

Constance Talbot threw her arms around me before I could even stand up from my pew in the chapel. Our heads bonked together, and she winced as she dropped her butt down onto the hard seat.

"Ow. Sorry. Got a little overexcited there," she said, rubbing furiously at her forehead. She was sun-kissed pink under all those freckles, and somehow over the summer she had tamed her somewhat frizz-prone red hair into a sleek, straight picture of perfection. She wore a white T-shirt and a big gray cable-knit cardigan over a plaid mini. Shafts of colorful light from the stained glass windows danced across her face.

"It's okay. You look amazing," I told her.

"I know. I found this new hair straightener that is a gift from the gods," she told me, swinging her long mane over her shoulder. "But *you* are, like, a surf babe! I would kill to be able to tan like that!"

"It comes from my mom's side. She's half Native American," I said.

"How cool! I never knew that!" Constance blurted. Then her brow creased. "Actually, I know nothing about your family."

"I don't usually talk about them," I agreed. But that, like many other things, had changed. "So, how was your summer?"

We had e-mailed all summer long, so I knew exactly how her months off had been, but still felt the need to ask. Her family had vacationed with Walt Whittaker's family up at the Cape. She and Whit had spent most nights stealing away to the beach or making out on the widow's walk at his family's compound while the waves crashed into the shore. Constance could be very poetic via e-mail.

"It was good!" she said brightly. "Except . . . I guess I didn't get an invitation to Billings."

I blinked as the chatter in the chapel grew to an almost deafening level. The place was starting to fill up. "That's right. I forgot about that."

Every spring the girls in Billings selected new members to replace the outgoing seniors. Last year the Billings alumnae had sent a letter—a directive, really—informing us that it would be inappropriate to hold a vote and issue invitations that year, considering all that had happened. That meant there were still six empty spots in the house. And I had no idea how anyone intended to fill them.

"Yeah, well, I guess I'm not worthy," she said wryly. "So who got in? You can tell me. I can take it."

"Actually, as far as I know, no one has gotten in. We haven't had a vote or anything. I guess I'll find out what's going on later. Maybe you still have a chance," I told her.

"You think?" Constance's eyes widened with hope, and I instantly regretted saying anything. Now she was going to be crushed all over again if she didn't get in.

"But don't freak out until I find out what's up," I warned her. "Honestly, after last year, I'm surprised anyone actually wants to get into Billings anymore," I added.

Not only was it partially true, but it would also give her something to rationalize on later if she didn't make the cut.

"Oh, please. That? Not even a murder could tarnish the mystique of Billings House," she blurted. Then slapped her hand over her mouth. "I'm sorry."

"No. It's okay," I said, forcing a smile. I wondered if she was right. If Thomas's death and Ariana's guilt—and my own near-death experience—had really left no lasting effect on anything. The idea made my insides squirm.

"No, really. I can't believe I said that," Constance continued. "You must think I'm totally—"

The sound of the heavy chapel doors closing cut her off, and the crowd fell silent. I was saved from having to comfort Constance any further for her verbal vomit. Diana reached over Constance's legs to nudge me and wave hello. As I leaned in, a tall, slim girl with light brown skin and long black hair slid into the last seat at the far end of the pew. She looked around uncertainly, then hugged her sheer turquoise wrap to her. With her gold braided thongs, skimpy dress, and dewy skin, she looked as if she'd just stepped off a plane from some exotic Caribbean locale and walked right into the chapel. She had to be new. Anyone who'd ever been in the Easton chapel before knew that even on the hottest days it was frigid in here. We'd all come prepared with fall sweaters. This girl must have been covered in goose bumps.

"Check out Miss Island Nation," Missy Thurber sneered behind me. Missy, of course, was wearing the tightest T-shirt possible, all the better to show off her massive chest, and her blond hair was done in a perfect French braid. Not perfect enough to distract from her tunnel-like nostrils, of course.

"Is she wearing *shells* for earrings?" Lorna Gross—Missy's ever-present worshipper—whispered back. Lorna was not down with originality. Every day, she donned almost the exact same outfit Missy had worn the day before. Like, in case you ever missed one of Missy's "ripped from *Teen Vogue*" fashion choices, you had a second chance to check it out on Lorna the following morning. Apparently yesterday Missy had worn a black jersey dress and diamond earrings, because that was what Lorna had on today.

I rolled my eyes and shot the new girl what I hoped was a welcoming smile. Unfortunately, she didn't see me. Her eyes were transfixed on two freshman boys lighting the lanterns at the front of the chapel. The new-year ritual had begun.

There was a loud rap on the chapel doors. A tall man with white hair and a full square face stood up from behind the lectern, his chin raised imperiously. Everything about him was stiff and pressed, from the collar of his white shirt to the perfectly straight cuffs on his gray suit pants. There was an American flag lapel pin tacked to his red power tie. He reminded me of some distinguished family patriarch from the low-rent soap opera Natasha's little sister had been addicted to all summer. The type of person who always knew what was going on around him, and approved of none of it. Whispers filled the room.

"Guess that's the new headmaster," I whispered to Constance.

"Headmaster Cromwell," she confirmed. "I heard he actually went here, like, a zillion years ago."

An Easton man. Interesting. My eyes were riveted on the head-master as he strode down the aisle, his hands straight down at his sides like one of the Queen's guard. He didn't look left or right. Felt no need to check out his new charges. He stopped at the door and spoke.

"Who requests entrance to this sacred place?" he asked.

"Eager minds in search of knowledge," came the reply.

"Then you are welcome," he said.

The doors opened, and in walked Cheyenne Martin and Lance Reagan, the sunlight pouring in behind them. This was the first I had seen of my housemate Cheyenne, and I was stunned by how beauti-ful she looked. Her blond hair had been cut into a pin-straight chin-length bob, and her skin was pale, smooth, and flawless. She wore just a hint of makeup—pink cheeks, pink lips, curled lashes—and looked every bit the preppy trust fund princess in her full-skirted dress and cropped cardigan. She and Lance kept their eyes trained on the lec-tern as they carried the traditional tomes up the aisle. As Cheyenne walked by the senior boys, I noticed Trey Prescott, handsome as ever in a crisp white shirt that set off his dark skin, staring straight ahead. Not so much as a glance in Cheyenne's direction. I could practically feel the chill coming off him. Guess that relationship hadn't survived the summer.

Cheyenne and Lance placed their books down on the lectern.

"Tradition, honor, excellence," they said in unison.

"Tradition, honor, excellence," we intoned, our voices filling the chapel.

The doors were closed again, and Headmaster Cromwell walked down the aisle and took his place at the lectern. He took a long moment to survey the rows and rows of pews, the expectantly upturned faces. From the slight sneer on his lips, he didn't seem all that impressed.

"Welcome, students, to a new year at Easton Academy. I am Headmaster Cromwell," he said, his voice low and commanding. "I am honored to have been chosen by the Easton Academy board of directors to take the helm and help usher you all into a new era. As of today, we put the past behind us. As of today, we are no longer a community torn by scandal and tragedy. We have all had our time to heal, and it is now that we must look to the future. A future that is bright with hope, with integrity, with knowledge, and with respect."

Constance and I shared an impressed glance.

"With this in mind, you should know that I will not accept anything other than the absolute best from the students of this academy. I will not brook insolence from my students. I will not tolerate indiscretion or immaturity. I will not allow any behavior whatsoever that could reflect negatively on this school. Hear me now, people, and hear me well. Things are going to change."

He said these last few words slowly, deliberately, as if hammering them into each and every adolescent brain one by one. So much for impressed. Now I was a tad freaked. From the looks on the faces around me, everyone felt the same.

"From this moment on, I expect each and every one of you to work toward a new Easton Academy," he said, his voice rising like a dictator's. "This school will hereafter be known as an institution that breeds character. That breeds decorum. And that turns out the very finest young men and women this country has to offer."

Suddenly, a loud, long farting noise filled the chapel. All the senior guys cracked up and shifted in their seats. I heard a cackle that could only belong to one person: Gage Coolidge.

The entire room tensed. My heart pounded as Headmaster Cromwell glowered toward the back of the chapel. He glanced right and nodded at a dark, shadowy figure in the corner behind him.

"Mr. White, if you please?" the headmaster asked.

A slim yet powerful-looking man with the sunken cheeks of a vampire and white-blond hair slipped down the side aisle and walked right over to Gage's pew. He leaned in and crooked a finger at Gage. It was all very grim reaper.

No one moved. Gage ducked his head and wagged it, like there was no way he was going anywhere. All the man did was lean even farther over the guy at the end of the pew and crook his finger again. Gage was beet red by this point. He shoved himself up and followed the creature out.

"Who. The hell. Is that?" Missy hissed behind me.

"The new Easton Academy henchman?" I suggested under my breath.

The chapel door slammed. I wasn't the only one who jumped.

"Now. Where were we?" Headmaster Cromwell asked. He seemed more chipper now, somehow. "Ah. Yes. This year we will be instituting a mentoring program. Several returning Easton students have been selected to mentor transfer students and the members of the incoming freshman class. When you are excused from here, kindly check your mailboxes to see if you have been so honored."

Missy and Lorna grumbled as many of my fellow students exchanged overwhelmed looks. This new headmaster was not messing around. The welcoming program lasted another thirty minutes, and for those thirty minutes, not a soul had the courage to move.

INTERESTING

"Can you believe that guy?" Missy fumed on our way out into the quad. Her nostrils somehow seemed even larger when she was angry. Like they were getting ready to breathe fire.

"I know. Like anything ever changes around here," Lorna added.

Well, she sure had. Lorna Gross had not only grown her dark hair out so that the frizzy curls formed less of a triangle, but she'd had an obvious nose job. She was almost pretty. Too bad she had no personality whatsoever to help her cause. *L210,417*

"I don't know. Everything just feels kind of different anyway. Doesn't it?" I asked, turning to Constance, Kiki, and Diana. I knew Missy and Lorna would answer me snidely, if at all.

"What are you on, Brennan?" Diana asked with a laugh. "Same old, same old, if you ask me."

"Maybe it just feels different because Noelle Lange isn't here casting her big bitch-slapping shadow over everyone," Missy said with a triumphant sneer.

Like Missy Thurber was even remotely good enough to look down on someone like Noelle Lange. But I knew that if anyone was happy to have Noelle gone, it was her. Last year Noelle had pretty much told Missy she had zero shot of getting into Billings—even though her mother had been a Billings girl. Now Missy's chances were wide open again. Unless I had anything to say about it.

"Did you ever hear from her this summer?" Constance asked me. "Or from any of them?"

Everyone eyed me expectantly. I, after all, was the only one among us who had any connection to the four girls who used to run Billings. Who used to run Easton, really. They were all looking to me as the person in the know. Someone special. The girl who had actually brushed with greatness. So I felt like a heel when I had to say:

"No. I haven't heard from any of them."

It wasn't as if I didn't want to hear from them. Wasn't as if I hadn't tried to track them down. But Noelle, Kiran, and Taylor had all changed their e-mails and their cell phone numbers. Every time I tried, I got an error message in my in-box or heard a nasal voice telling me the number was no longer in service. After a while I had to grow some pride and accept the fact that they had moved on. Without me. Natasha maintained that I should be glad to be rid of them. And maybe I should have been on some level. But it still hurt to be so easily and callously cut out.

Missy scoffed and rolled her eyes and kept walking, so Lorna did the same. I wanted to conk their heads together, but held my hands behind my back instead.

"I heard Ariana's in some mental facility in, like, the Southwest or something," Diana said. "Total maximum security."

I'd heard that one, too, but I'd heard it was in upstate New York. Every time I thought of Ariana, I pictured her in a straitjacket, her light blue eyes staring out some window as she contemplated her next move, Hannibal Lecter–style. Then I'd have to shake my head to clear the image and the awful tingling sensation it gave me down my spine.

"Taylor Bell's living in Portugal," Lorna said.

"No. It was Prague," Missy shot back.

"Nuh-uh," Kiki said, speaking up for the first time—loudly since her iPod was blasting into her ears. "Rehab."

"What? No. Taylor didn't even like to drink that much," I said.

"Pills," Kiki said seriously. "It's always the quiet ones." Ironic, since she herself was among the taciturn.

"Well, I know for a fact that Kiran's living in Paris and modeling," Diana said. "I saw her new CK billboard on the Champs-Élysées over the summer, and my mom knows the photographer. He said she's totally professional now. No partying. No late nights. No crazy diets. Just shows up for work and goes home to read."

"Now I *know* that is a lie," I joked.

"I just think it's weird that none of them came back," Constance said as we reached the break in the path between Billings and Pemberly, one of the junior and senior girls' dorms. "I mean, unless they're all in jail or something, why wouldn't they come back?"

"Uh, because of the extreme personal humiliation?" Missy said sarcastically. She studied the end of her braid before flicking it over her shoulder. "They're a bunch of psychos anyway. We're better off without them."

My fingers curled into a fist behind my back. "What's the matter with you?"

"Problem?" Missy asked, flicking her eyes over me. "I'd think you of all people would want to see Noelle and her posse burn at the stake. They did murder your boyfriend."

"No, *they* didn't. Ariana did. The rest of them made a mistake," I told her, barely holding back my fury. Even though some small part of me agreed with some small part of what she said, I felt that she was the last person who had any right saying it. "They were my friends."

"Nice friends," Missy said derisively. "I guess that's why you never liked me? Because I'm not a sociopath?"

"You little—"

"Oh. My. God," Lorna interrupted me. "Speaking of coming back—"

I whipped around, half-expecting to see Noelle or Taylor or Kiran. But no. The girl walking toward us had sharp features, milk-white skin, and very long, perfectly straight and glossy black hair. Her coal-black eyes looked us over as she walked by, as if studying a new and unattractive species. Her look was so cold I almost shivered under the blazing late-summer sun. No way this girl had been at Easton last year. I would have remembered her.

"Hi, Ivy!" Diana said brightly. "How have you—"

She didn't get to finish her question because three words in, the girl was already out of earshot, passing us by like she hadn't heard a thing.

"Bitch," Missy said under her breath.

"Whore," Lorna added.

I stared after the girl until she had disappeared through the back door of Pemberly, the tiff with Missy the Nostril Girl forgotten. Things had just gotten interesting.

EVERY LAST INCH

"Her name's Ivy Slade," Josh told me, slipping his fingers between mine. "She used to go here, but last year she never showed. Now she's back. She and Taylor Bell used to room together back in the day."

Okay. Now I was *definitely* intrigued.

"How do you know all this, exactly?" I asked. He, after all, had only been at Easton a year. Just like me. I tried to work the combination on my mailbox with my left hand, since he was holding my right. It wasn't entirely working.

"Gage gossips like a girl," he replied. He held up my hand and kissed the back of each finger, one by one. "He said they used to have a thing. Like, a serious thing."

"She and Gage," I said dubiously. "I don't see him in a serious relationship."

"Did I say relationship? I meant sex. They had serious sex," Josh clarified. "All over campus. Or so he says."

I shuddered. Well, that explained Lorna's "whore" remark. "Okay. Too much information. Moving on."

I didn't need to hear any details of Gage and Ivy's Easton Sex Tour, but I filed the info about her and Taylor away for future reference. Maybe they had been good friends. Maybe they still were. Maybe this Ivy person even knew where Taylor had ended up. After everything we'd been through together, I was curious to know what the Billings Girls were doing with themselves. Even if they, as evidenced by their total silence, had zero interest in me.

"Okay." Josh dropped my right hand, took my left, and started kissing those fingers as well.

"What are you doing?" I asked him with a laugh.

"I have this whole plan to kiss all your body parts before the end of the first week," Josh said matter-of-factly.

"*All* of them?" I said, a blush working its way up my neck. The Josh I knew wasn't normally so forward.

Josh smiled playfully. "Well, whichever ones you'll allow me to."

"Ah." That was more like Josh. I leaned toward him and touched my lips to his.

"You two are so making my first gallery show!" a booming voice announced.

We sprang away from each other. Tiffany Goulbourne raced over, her ubiquitous camera in hand, all smiles.

"Did you just take our picture?" I asked her.

"Yes. And it's one you're going to want to show the grandkids one day." She gave Josh and me the double air kiss she gave everyone, then leaned back to inspect me head-to-toe. "Reed, my friend. You just got even *more* photogenic this summer. That hair! That skin!"

"Look who's talking," I replied.

Tiffany was a resident of Billings House whom I'd gotten to know much better during the second semester of last year, after all the insanity had died down. She was tall and lithe, with ebony skin and short cropped hair. Could have been a model herself, no doubt, but she preferred to be behind the camera. All the time. No matter where she was or what she was doing, she had a lens on her, whether it was an old-school 35-millimeter or a teeny, tiny digital. One was never safe from her keen eye. She was like our very own paparazzo. Except everyone loved her.

"Yeah, right," she said, blushing. "You have to let me photograph you this year. You have to."

"We'll see," I told her, amused.

Tiff had spent half the spring semester trying to coax everyone we knew to pose in various lights for her final art project. As much as I enjoyed the girl's positive energy, I'd had enough attention for one year and had found various hiding places in the house to avoid her. Cheyenne had, of course, ended up being the star of her pictorial. For which Tiffany had inevitably received an A.

"Oh. There's London and Vienna. First Twin Cities pic of the year!" And just like that, Tiffany was off again, dodging through the hordes of freshmen checking out their mailboxes for the first time, ready to snap London Simmons and Vienna Clark—the bodacious Twin Cities—in all their freshly tanned glory.

"Well? Let's see what you've got," Josh said, nodding at my post office box.

I quickly opened it and pulled out the folded slip of blue paper inside. I'd seen a few other people with them, groaning over their contents, so I already knew I'd been pegged. The short typewritten note read:

> Congratulations, Ms. Brennan. You have been selected as an Easton Academy Mentor. Your Advisee is:
>
> Sabine DuLac, Junior (transfer); Residence, Billings House
>
> If you should have any questions, please contact Mrs. Naylor, Head of Guidance.

"That can't be right," I said.

"What? Don't think you're trustworthy enough to take a young fledgling under your wing?" Josh asked as I slammed the mailbox door.

Josh had not been saddled with a newbie, even though he was one of Easton's best and brightest. My guess was the administration decided to give him a pass, considering how stressful his junior year had been. When your roommate and best friend gets murdered and you're mistakenly jailed for the crime, a pass is wholeheartedly deserved. Although, it seemed, there was no such amnesty for the victim's girlfriend. But then, Cromwell was all business, and a roommate has an official Easton connection whereas a girlfriend does not. At least this year Josh was rooming with Trey. That guy was the epitome of the all-American boy, jogging around campus every morning, lead-ing the soccer team in goals scored, being recruited by every school in the country. He wouldn't be dealing drugs, coming home drunk, and inspiring people to hurt him.

Not that I blamed Thomas for what had happened to him, but let's just say that a year's worth of perspective had opened my eyes to the fact that he wasn't a person who was easy to get along with.

"No, it just says she lives in Billings," I told Josh, holding up the slip. "We haven't even chosen new housemates. At least I don't think we have. Unless they did it without me or something." Which, consid-ering my experiences with the Billings Girls, wouldn't actually have shocked me all that much.

Josh shrugged and grabbed my hand again. "They probably just made a mistake." He kissed my pinkie, then my ring finger, and a skittering surge of attraction rushed right through me. Huh. Sensi-tive ring finger.

"You're going to have to stop that," I said under my breath. "I'm a mentor now. I have an image to uphold." I looked into his eyes, all flirtatious.

"Let me see this," he said, taking the slip out of my hands. "Sabine DuLac? Sounds like French royalty or something. Probably not too easily shocked."

He was just leaning in to kiss me when London and Vienna, the Twin Cities themselves, rushed by. They had matching tans, matching highlights, and their matching mega-breasts were spilling over the necklines of very similar sundresses.

"Reed! We have to go! We have a house meeting before first period, and we're already late. Cheyenne's gonna be so pissed."

All our classes had been delayed and shortened for the day so we could get settled. But leave it to Cheyenne to commandeer our time for her own purposes instead. I sighed. Probably best that I leave now anyway, before Josh and I started something entirely inappropriate in broad daylight in the middle of a crowded post office. I had a feeling Cromwell wasn't the type to turn the other cheek when it came to PDA.

"I guess I have to go," I told him, lifting a shoulder.

I gave him a quick kiss on the lips, forced myself to pull away, and turned to follow my housemates. Josh grabbed my wrist and stopped me. He pulled me to him and turned me around so that my back was to the mailboxes.

"Josh. What if a teacher—"

He cut me off with his lips, pressing up against me and kissing me so urgently, I forgot all about the faculty and the potential ramifications. Even stopped feeling all the tiny little metal knobs pressing into my back. I felt that kiss everywhere. In every last inch of my body.

"Okay. Now you can go," Josh said, backing up with a semicocky smile.

I blinked at him, my eyelids heavy. "Which way again?"

Josh laughed and turned me by the shoulders toward the door, where London and Vienna waited, smirking at me.

"Guess you're happy to be back, huh?" London teased as I tottered toward her.

"Yeah." She had no idea. "Definitely."

NEW RULES

"Welcome back, everyone!"

Cheyenne stood at the head of a long, polished wood table that had taken over the entire parlor on the first floor of Billings House, her manicured fingertips pressed into its surface. All the comfy chairs and couches were gone, and the flat-screen TV had been pushed into the back corner. In the center of the table were six small pink jewelry boxes, stacked into a pyramid. At each of the ten chairs around the table—one at each head and four per side—was another pink jewelry box, a white pad of paper, a silver pen, and a place card. I saw my name right away, at the last seat on the right side—as far away from Cheyenne as I could get without being directly across from her. My name, just like the others, was written in pink calligraphy.

"Find your seats! We have a lot to cover in not a lot of time!" Cheyenne announced, waving us in.

The other girls, who had been chatting in little groups around the room, took their chairs. I slid into mine, and Rose Sakowitz, Cheyenne's diminutive, red-haired roommate from last year, took the chair at the end of the table. She had a bit more meat on her bones than she had last year. Comforting, since she had always looked as if she could blow away in a stiff wind. But she was still probably rocking a size zero. Her yellow skirt was so tiny, I could have used it as a headband.

"Hi, Reed," she whispered with a smile and a quick wave.

"Hi," I whispered back. "Good to see you."

"You, too. How was your summer?" Rose asked.

"Ladies! If you don't mind?" Cheyenne snapped.

Oh. So that was how this was going to go. Ever since last spring when Cheyenne had taken the whole sorority thing and really run with it, she had been on a power trip from hell. She had run for president unopposed and created a cabinet that included London and Vienna as co-social chairs, Rose as philanthropy chair, and Tiffany as historian (which basically meant Tiff was a glorified scrapbooker). With her new regime in place, Cheyenne had made sure that no moment of free time was left unoccupied. There had been teas and parties and fundraisers and day trips. Whenever we weren't studying, we were bonding. And it had been fun. Most of the time. Except for when Cheyenne was cracking her whip. What was that saying about absolute power corrupting absolutely? Cheyenne could have that stamped across her forehead. Sometimes I missed the old semisweet Cheyenne from last Christmas, but the more we hung out, the more I realized that these were Cheyenne's true colors. At the end of the fall semester she'd

merely put on a happy face in her effort to overthrow Noelle. Now that
Noelle was truly gone, she was back to her bitchy self, and only every
once in a while did Cool Cheyenne come shining through.

"First of all, welcome back to Billings," Cheyenne began as Tiffany
snapped her photo. "I hope you all had fabulous summer breaks. I'd
love to hear all about the European tours and the trips to the Cape, but
right now we have some business to attend to." She grinned and lifted
her palms in the air. "Now I know you're all dying to find out what's in
those little boxes, so go to it!"

London squealed and snatched up her pink box like it was steak
and she, a rabid dog. I had actually forgotten about mine. I pulled it
closer and cracked it open. Inside was a tiny letter *B* on a thin gold
chain, with diamonds and in script. All the girls around me oohed and
aahed as they fastened them around each other's necks.

"Cheyenne! These are so yum!" Vienna trilled, helping London on
with hers.

"They're perfect," London added. "Now everyone will know who's
a Billings Girl and who's not."

As if they don't already.

"Thanks, Shy. You're so gen!" Portia Ahronian trilled. She added
the necklace to the five or six gold chains she always wore around
her neck, which offset her olive complexion gorgeously. I had never
gotten to know Portia all that well last year, but I had witnessed her
stellar partying skills and noted her serious jewelry fetish. She was
also quite the fashionista and would probably take Kiran's place as
head couture monger of Billings, now that Kiran was apparently an

expatriate. Portia also had a penchant for shortening words, which drove me insane. Talking to her was like talking to a text message.

"Don't thank me. Thank the Billings Alumnae Fund," Cheyenne said. I noticed she already had a *B* necklace shimmering against her milky skin. Was it just me, or was hers slightly larger than all the others?

"The Billings Alumnae Fund?" I asked.

"God, Reed. Did you pick up nothing last year?" Cheyenne asked with a laugh.

"All the Billings alumnae contribute to it every month," Rose explained. "It's how we paid for all the parties and trips last year."

Interesting. I'd never heard of the alumnae fund before. But then, I had been kept in the dark about a lot of things last year. Rose offered to help me with my chain, and I turned to let her fasten it. The *B* felt cold and delicate against my chest.

"We have to take a picture of all of us with our necklaces on!" Tiffany announced. "Get together everyone!"

"After the meeting," Cheyenne said bluntly. Those who had started to get up fell back into their seats. "We have a lot to cover," Cheyenne continued. She pulled a pink plastic folder out of her Kate Spade bag and unwound the fastening string. "Normally we choose new housemates in the spring, with the aid of the outgoing seniors, and extend our invitations then. But considering all that went on last year, it seemed a bit gauche."

And we were ordered not to do it, but go ahead and make it seem like it was your own sense of propriety that forestalled this whole thing.

"Now we're in the position of having to fill the house and having to do it quickly. But I'm sure we're all up to the task." She handed a stack of papers to Tiffany on her right and Vienna on her left. "Find the pages with your name on them and pass the others on," she instructed. "These are all the current juniors. We will need to choose six girls from the more than one hundred possibles."

I glanced at the pyramid of boxes in the center of the table. Six girls. Six more necklaces.

"You will each be responsible for vetting at least ten prospective Billings Girls," Cheyenne continued.

"Vetting?" I asked as the pages were dropped in front of me. I noted the first name with dismay: Lorna Gross. Along with her name and her unfortunate sophomore class picture was a list of all her vitals—her birthday, primary residence, final grades from last year, clubs and sports, plus paragraphs about all her family members and her parents' income. There was even a rundown of where they summered and vacationed during winter break for the past ten years. How this information was obtained, I had no idea. I turned to the second page and smiled. Kiki Rosen. As far as I was concerned, Kiki—straight-A student and cool person that she was—was in as of that moment. And, holy crap, was that really how much her family was worth?

"First, you will make an appointment to sit down with each of your girls and conduct an interview. Make sure they're Billings material. That they really want it," Cheyenne said, strolling around the table imperiously. "Second, and more important, you will keep an eye on them. See how they conduct themselves when they think no one is watching. That is when their true characters will be revealed."

My laughter filled the otherwise silent room. Every person at the table stared me down.

"She's not kidding," Rose said.

No way. "You want me to spy on these girls?"

Cheyenne flattened her lips like I'd just jammed a lemon drop into her mouth. "This is how it's done. This is how it's always been done."

"With one exception," Portia said, casting a haughty glance in my direction.

Right. Me. As always, the black sheep.

"Bygones," Cheyenne said with a wave of her hand. "But it does bring up a good point. Considering all that happened last year, it is of the utmost importance that we get the *right* girls this year. We have to buff the tarnished Billings image. Show the world that those girls are not indicative of the type of women we want to be."

Can I barf now?

"Um, Cheyenne? What about Ivy?" Rose asked.

A skitter of anticipation raced down my spine.

"What *about* Ivy?" Cheyenne snapped.

Okay. Clearly no love lost there.

"Well, she would've been in Billings no Q last year if she hadn't gone MIA," Portia said, inspecting her nails. "Should we re-extend the invite?"

"No. We want juniors only. The whole point is to guide the future of the house, not take someone new who will be out of here in a few months," Cheyenne said. "Besides, did no one hear a word I just said? I don't really think Ivy Slade is the right sort of girl."

There were many knowing glances and a few snickers. Rose, however, did not look happy.

"We will choose our new housemates from among the junior class, and we will choose wisely," Cheyenne said. "It's up to us to ensure the future of this house."

Out in the lobby, the front door opened. We all looked around, wondering who was missing. It sounded as if a crowd had just walked through the door. Seconds later Headmaster Cromwell appeared, practically filling the parlor doorway. He looked down the table with obvious distaste.

"Ladies."

"Headmaster! Hello," Cheyenne greeted him uncertainly.

He stepped aside slightly. "Come in. Let's not be shy," he said over his shoulder.

There was stunned silence as six girls walked into the room and lined up by the lace curtains at the front window. Lorna Gross, Missy Thurber, Constance Talbot, Kiki Rose, Astrid Chou—who as far as I knew was Cheyenne's friend from Barton School—and the new girl from the chapel. Miss Island Nation, as Lorna had called her.

"Ladies, allow me to introduce your new housemates," the headmaster said with a curt nod.

"What!?" Cheyenne blurted. Screeched, actually.

The headmaster eyed her with disdain. "These girls are among the elite in the junior class. They have been selected by the board of directors and have been granted the honor of residing in Billings House."

Tiffany snapped their picture. Everyone else around me looked appalled. He had to be kidding. They couldn't just decide who was going to live in Billings. That wasn't how it was done. But then I noticed Constance's expression. She looked like a five-year-old who'd just been dropped off at Willy Wonka's Chocolate Factory. That lessened the sting. At least enough to make me smile.

"Headmaster Cromwell." Cheyenne's voice sounded weak as she tried to regain her senses. She gripped the back of Tiffany's chair and faced him. "I'm sorry, but the women of Billings House have always selected our own housemates. It's one of the privileges of living here. That's how it's always been done. For the past eighty years."

The headmaster eyed Cheyenne with a look of barely veiled disdain. "Ms. Martin, is it?"

"Yes, sir." She was clearly pleased that her reputation preceded her.

"I heard all about you from Dean Marcus," he said. "Including the little deal you made with him last year to get you and your friends off campus during the holidays."

Cheyenne's smile faltered a bit.

"Well, let me make something perfectly clear to you," he continued. "*I* do not make deals with students. I tell you how it's going to be, and your response is, 'Yes, sir. Thank you, sir. Good day, sir.'"

Every single one of us was frozen in place.

"As of today, this house will no longer be run like a sorority," he continued with a sniff. He reached over Rose's shoulder and picked up her place card, which he glanced over quickly before flicking it back on the table with obvious disgust. London pulled hers to her as if to hide it. "I've heard about your rituals and initiations. That all stops now. This is a dormitory. A living space. That is all."

I felt a dart of pain shoot through me and knew that the others probably felt the degradation even more acutely. Living in Billings was supposed to mean something. It meant something to all of us. And he'd just snatched that away and insulted us in the process.

"Do you have anything to say to that, Ms. Martin?" he asked, lifting his chin.

"I . . ."

"Yes, sir . . . ," he prompted her.

Wow. This was humiliating. Big time, boob-out-of-bathing-suit humiliating. Cheyenne cleared her throat and cast her eyes at the ground.

"Yes, sir. Thank you, sir. Good day, sir."

At least she put some sarcastic emphasis on the last *sir*. That was something.

"I'll leave you all to get to know each other," the headmaster said. Then he turned on his heel and strode out.

For a long moment, nobody moved. Cheyenne's ire could have incinerated the whole room.

"That man needs a good shagging," Astrid joked, her British accent somehow making the joke funnier.

Everyone laughed nervously. Everyone except Cheyenne.

"They can't do this to us," she said, her voice like ice.

"I think they just did," Tiffany replied.

"No. This is my senior year. They can't just change everything now," Cheyenne ranted. "They just can't. I've been looking forward to this for my entire Easton career. They can't just bring us these random people and expect that to be it!"

"Cheyenne," Rose scolded, jumping up. She glanced at the six girls by the window apologetically, then grabbed Cheyenne's wrist and pulled her into the corner, talking to her in low tones. Vienna and London quickly joined them.

I glanced at the other girls at the table, who looked just as dumb-struck and unsure as I felt. But it couldn't have been half of what Constance and the new girls were feeling. I couldn't just let them stand there all uncertain and out of place. I got up and gave Constance an awkward hug.

"Congratulations!" I told her. I couldn't think of anything else to say. A few of the other Billings Girls followed my lead and roused themselves to talk to our visitors. Gradually, chatter filled the room, drowning out Cheyenne and the others.

"What's wrong with Cheyenne?" Constance whispered. "Does she really not want us here?"

"She wants to vote, like always," I said. "She wants the power to decide who lives here. But what's she going to do? The headmaster seemed pretty serious. If he says you're living here, you're living here."

"I don't believe it. I'm in Billings!" Constance said, wide-eyed.

"Just wait till you see what's in those boxes," I told her, glancing at the table.

Constance glanced at the empty pink boxes strewn all over the place, then looked around the room, practically drooling as she noticed the diamond *B*s everywhere.

"Omigod! Am I going to get one?" she asked, reaching out to touch my pendant.

I shrugged. "Looks to me like all the Billings girls have one, so . . ."

Constance quietly squealed and I moved on to Astrid, whom I'd met at Cheyenne's Christmas party last year. True to her original fashion sense, she was wearing a strapless dress with postage stamps all over it, yellow flats, and a flower in her short, shaggy hair.

"Reed! It's so nice to see a familiar face," she said.

"I know! What are you doing here?" I asked. "What happened to Barton?"

"Caught me smoking behind the gymnasium one too many times, didn't they?" Her brown eyes gleamed with mischief. "But no matter. I always wanted to come here anyway."

I introduced her to Kiki and Constance, then turned to the new girl who stood in the corner, her hands behind her back, shyly observing the room.

"Sabine, right?" I said.

Her face lit up, if possible rendering it even more beautiful. "Yes. How did you know?"

Her English was slightly accented. French, as Josh predicted. I pulled the blue slip out of my back pocket and handed it to her. "I'm Reed. Looks like I'm supposed to show you around."

"Oh, *merci*! I'm so happy to meet you," Sabine said, hand to chest. "This place is a bit intimidating, no?"

I smiled. "Just a tad."

"No! Forget it!" Cheyenne blurted from across the room. "This is not acceptable!" She turned to the six newcomers. "You! Sit!" she ordered, pointing her finger at the table. "The rest of you, my room. Now."

She swept the six remaining jewelry boxes up in her arms as if she was afraid the new girls might pilfer them, then stormed out of the parlor, the rest of the Billings Girls trailing behind her. I looked at Sabine and the others with an apology in my eyes and sighed.

"Okay. Maybe more than a tad."

CREATIVE THINKING

"They have no right to do this! What were they thinking?" Cheyenne ranted, pacing back and forth in her huge single room. She had taken Noelle and Ariana's old room again this year, but somehow had managed to secure it all to herself. It was still weird to be in here without Noelle's ridiculous mess on one side and Ariana's OCD primness on the other, but Cheyenne had done all she could to make it her own. She had a double bed set up near the bay window, two dressers, a huge desk, an ornate vanity table, and a sitting area. Plus room enough for all ten Billings residents to hang out at once. Everything in sight was white, pink, or mossy green—the bedspread, the chair coverings, the throw pillows, the fresh-cut flowers in the bay window. It was like she was living in an English garden. "I mean, Lorna Gross? I don't care if she did take a private jet to Switzerland for her nose job. She's still Lorna Gross!"

"And did you see that one girl's shoes?" Portia said, her eyes practically crossing as she inspected a lock of hair for split ends. "Wrong!"

I looked at Tiffany, confused. Which girl was she talking about? Tiff simply shrugged.

"Well, at least Astrid got in," I said, trying to find a tack that would placate Cheyenne. "Aren't you two, like, best friends?"

Cheyenne leveled me with a glare. "We *know* each other," she corrected. "And that is so not the point."

"But she is right. Transfer students never get into Billings," Rose piped in from her seat on one of Cheyenne's upholstered chairs. "Maybe the board did you a favor."

"Are you kidding me? How am I the only one here who's upset? This is an affront to all of us," Cheyenne said. "They don't know what it takes to be in Billings. They can't just suddenly decide who's worthy. Each and every one of us was carefully selected by women who have lived here, who know what it's about. The board of directors has no clue, and Headmaster Cromwell certainly doesn't."

"Yeah, but Kiki and Constance are both cool. Kiki got First Honors twice last year, and Constance landed editor-in-chief of the *Chronicle* even though she's only a junior," I pointed out. "And I'm not the biggest fan of Lorna or Missy's either, but Missy's a Billings legacy. Wouldn't she have automatically gotten in anyway?"

"The girl has a point," Tiffany said, toying with her camera.

"But it doesn't change the fact that Evil HC just swooped in here and stripped us of our rights," Portia said. Her bangle bracelets jangled as she crossed her arms over her chest. "The man's an alum. He should know better."

"Exactly," Cheyenne said, her eyes lighting up now that someone was getting her back.

Unreal. Somehow I was still shocked by the Billings ego.

"Yeah. And now we don't get to spy on the prospects." London pouted. "I was so looking forward to that part. I even got binoculars," she said, producing a sleek set of silver binocs from her leather Prada bag.

"See?" Cheyenne said, lifting a hand like this was such a heinous affront. "London didn't even get to use her binoculars."

"Well, she did already use them on Ketlar this morning," Vienna joked, earning snickers all around. She and London slapped hands, their identical French manicures clicking together, looking quite pleased with themselves. I hoped Josh's room wasn't facing theirs.

"Look, the way I see it, all this means is we don't have to do all the work," I said. "They already did it for us."

Honestly, I didn't like having my say in the matter taken away much more than anyone else did. But I had a feeling that my Billings sisters, with their indefinable standards, might not have accepted Constance, and I did not want to see that girl heartbroken. I couldn't imagine how crushed I would have been if on the same day I'd been invited into Billings, I had then been summarily tossed out. All I wanted to do was accept the decree and move on.

Cheyenne's eyes flashed. "Laziness is no excuse for giving up everything that Billings stands for, Reed," she snapped. "Not that I'd expect you to understand that," she added under her breath.

My face burned hot. "Excuse me?"

"What? Oh, nothing," she said with a sweet smile.

As irritated as I was, I didn't feel like getting into a knock-down, drag-out fight with Cheyenne, so I chose to ignore her dig and focus on the current issue. "I don't want to give up everything Billings stands for either, but what are we going to do? I say we just give the new girls their necklaces and get on with our year."

There was a general murmur of assent that boosted my confidence.

"Uh, no. I don't think so. They don't just *get* necklaces," Cheyenne said, cutting us all off. "We have no way of knowing if those girls are even Billings material."

"Well, it's too late now," Rose said with a shrug. "They're moving in. They're gonna have to be Billings material."

My thoughts exactly. Why couldn't I have said it first?

Cheyenne's blue eyes narrowed. "Not necessarily."

Oh, God. I didn't like that tone. A very familiar skitter of nervousness raced down my spine.

"Oooh, what're you thinking?" Vienna asked.

Apparently, Vienna *did* like that tone.

"I'm thinking we can still test them. Just because they're living under our roof, that doesn't mean they can't still be vetted," Cheyenne said. "We'll come up with a task for them to perform, and those who pass, fine. But those who don't . . ."

A few of the girls eyed one another conspiratorially. I, however, was a blank.

"Those who don't, what?" I asked.

"Well, we'll deal with that when the time comes," Cheyenne said, crossing over to pat me on the shoulder like a little girl.

"I don't get it," I said, trying to stave off whatever heinousness these girls had in mind. "The headmaster said they're living here. There's nothing we can do."

"Oh, there's always something we can do, Reed," Cheyenne said with a beatific smile. "You just need a little creative thinking."

NEEDED

When I walked into my room after our brief and irritating meeting, Sabine was zipping her empty suitcase closed and stashing it under her bed. Her sheets were simple and white, and her closet was only half-filled with exotic, flimsy-looking clothing in all sorts of bright colors. Flat sandals lined the floor along with one pair of sneakers. There were three candles on the table next to her bed and two photos. A picture of her and two friends in bathing suits, standing in a simple bamboo frame, and a larger print of Sabine in a school uniform, hugging a woman who had to be her mother. This was framed in silver.

"That's it?" I asked.

She lifted a small stack of hardcover books off her bed and placed them on her desk next to a silver Apple laptop. "That is all."

"Wow. And I thought I was a minimalist."

I crossed over to my bed and sat down, facing her. She looked around at her things and shrugged her slim shoulders. "I wore a uniform at my old school, so I didn't need much. And I suppose sweaters and winter clothes take up more room, but I don't have those things yet. Do you know where I could buy a good coat?"

"I'm not the person you want to ask," I told her with a sardonic smile. "Portia or Cheyenne, maybe. If you follow my advice, you'll be so horribly last year," I joked, putting on a snobby voice.

"Cheyenne? The girl with the temper?" Sabine shuddered. "No thank you."

I smiled. "So, where are you from that you don't need a winter coat?"

"Martinique," she said, pacing over to the window to gaze out at the mountains. "Have you ever been?"

"Can't say that I have," I replied with a private smile. Actually, I'd never even been on a plane before, but she didn't need to know that.

"It's a small island. Very hot. My family lives in a house on the beach, so I grew up in the sun and not wearing much of anything," she said with a wistful smile.

"Sounds nice. Why come here?" I asked.

"I've always wanted to see what it is like to live in the States," she said simply.

Yeah. Easton Academy wasn't really going to give her a snapshot of a normal U.S. existence.

"It is strange, though. Being here," she said with a sigh, staring out the window.

"How so?" I asked.

Aside from the obvious.

"I was so excited to come here. Life at home can be . . . compli-cated," she told me with a small, almost apologetic smile. "I couldn't wait to get away. But now that I'm here . . ."

"You miss home," I finished for her.

"Exactement," she replied.

I recalled that feeling. Last year I had sat in my room at Bradwell completely confused as to how I could possibly be homesick, what with my brother off at school and my mother catatonic in bed. And yet, there I was, verge-of-tears girl. I had, however, gotten over that fairly quickly, what with all the hazing, confusion, and abject fear that had soon come my way.

"You get used to it," I told her.

"Really?" she looked at me hopefully, and I felt a pang in my chest. This girl needed a friend. Maybe Cromwell's mentor idea was a good one.

"I promise," I replied.

"Good. I'll just think of this as an adventure," Sabine said firmly. "It's like a different world, anyway. All the stone and brick and hills and trees. And the ceremony this morning? Like a scene from a novel." Her eyes gleamed with excitement.

"Yeah. It is pretty cool," I agreed, remembering the warm rush I'd gotten the first time I'd seen it. That feeling of being part of some-thing bigger. The optimistic expectation that it had inspired inside me. I could only hope that Sabine would have a better first semester than I'd had.

But then, how could it possibly be any worse?

My computer let out a beep, and I got up to check my e-mail.
"Sorry."

"No problem," she said lightly.

I blinked when I saw the address. DaMcCafferty@yale.edu.

Dash? Dash McCafferty was e-mailing me? I felt an odd flutter of
excitement in my chest and told myself to chill. I clicked it open.

> Hey Reed,
>
> Just wanted to check in and see how Easton is doing.
> Yale is just what I expected. A lot of people seem over-
> whelmed, but I think Easton may have been more difficult.
> My roommate's a tool, but after living with Gage, I think I
> can deal. Write back when you get a chance.
>
> —Dash

"Oooh. Someone's blushing," Sabine said, walking over. "Who's
it from?"

I wasn't blushing. I couldn't be blushing. Just because Dash and I
had shared that one freaky maybe-moment over the summer . . .

"Just a friend," I told her. "He graduated last year."

"Oh? *Un petit ami?*" she teased.

What the heck? Did I look flustered or something? Maybe I was a
tad excited, but only because I was surprised that Dash would bother
keeping in touch with me. That was all.

"Uh, no. He was a friend's boyfriend," I told her.

Was? Is? I had no idea. Dash had come to the Vineyard with his family for a wedding in August, and Natasha and I had hung out with him for a few days. But the whole time we were together, he didn't mention Noelle once. Taking his lead, we hadn't brought her up either, even though we'd both been dying to know what he knew. Still, it seemed cruel to mention it. How could he have possibly been dealing with the idea that his girlfriend had any sort of a hand—however inadvertent—in his best friend's death?

And then, that moment had happened. After the wedding Dash had shown up at the Old Fisherman—the restaurant I'd worked at all summer—slightly tipsy, his blond hair disheveled by the wind, still wearing his tux, but with the tie adorably loosened. I'd been closing up the porch tables on my own, and he had pitched right in, helping me stack the chairs and move everything toward the wall to protect them from the wind, as I did every night. He told me stories about all the uptight snobs at the wedding, and we ended up out there for an hour, laughing and talking as we looked out over the water.

"I wish you'd been there," he said, leaning his thick forearms on the railing. "It would've been a lot more fun."

My heart skipped a surprised beat at the way he was looking at me. "Yeah. Sounds like good people watching," I replied, trying to make light.

"I can't believe I'm going to Yale in a few weeks," he said.

"Yeah. College. It's so huge," I replied.

"No. Not that. I just wish . . . I wish I could go back to Easton. Do senior year all over. I would do so many things differently," he told me in that earnest way of his.

"Like what?"

"Like . . ." He looked me in the eye in this searching way, and I froze. Even though I knew what he was thinking, even though I'd just talked to Josh from Germany two hours before, I didn't move. This was Dash McCafferty. He was almost mind-bogglingly gorgeous. And I swear, when he tipped his head toward mine, there was a moment of insanity in which I was going to kiss him back.

And then I remembered I had a conscience. I backed off. Cleared my throat, acted like nothing had happened, and so did he. By the next day I was absolutely positive I had imagined the whole thing. Or that I hadn't, but he'd been more drunk than I'd thought and hadn't known what he was doing. That he'd somehow thought in his bleary condition that I was Noelle. Okay, she was *Vogue*-level gorgeous and I was me, but we both had brown hair, similar heights, and athletic bods. It was possible. Whatever the case had been, I hadn't seen or heard from him again until this moment, even though his family had spent two more days on the island.

"Oh. Well, tell him your new roommate said hello," Sabine said before moving back to arrange her things.

I nervously started to type a quick response, my fingers shaking ever so slightly after recalling that summer night so vividly. Taking Dash's sort of detached lead, I filled him in on the new headmaster, the situation at Billings, and the mentor program. I had just hit SEND when Constance burst into our room. If there was one thing she was good for, it was total distraction.

"Omigod! Reed! The view from my and Kiki's room is *so* gorgeous!" she rambled. "I can't believe I'm in Billings! I can't believe it!"

"Why are you so excited?" Sabine asked, looking up from a turquoise T-shirt she was folding. "Is this place special somehow?"

"You have no idea!" Constance trilled. "This is the most exclusive dorm on campus. They don't let just anyone live here."

Except this year.

"So when do we get our necklaces?" Constance reached out to touch my diamond *B*. "Did you notice that Cheyenne's is bigger than everyone else's?"

I knew it!

"I can't wait to get mine!"

"Calm down, Constance. Take a breath," I told her, laughing guiltily. Little did Constance know that she wasn't actually a Billings Girl yet. At least not as far as certain people were concerned. "I'm sure you'll get one eventually."

Especially since I'm planning to help you and Sabine pass whatever stupid test Cheyenne comes up with.

"Oh, God. I can't wait! I have to call Whit! He's going to be so happy for me! He told me I could still get in, but I didn't believe him. He was just being Whit, you know? You know how he is. Anyway—"

Constance whipped out her cell phone to call Whittaker, who was now a Harvard man. She turned away from me and Sabine as she greeted Whit and squealed into her phone. I shot Sabine an apologetic glance, but she just smiled back.

No eye-rolling. No judging. Which were the reactions Constance often got around Easton. Sabine really was going to get a culture shock at this school.

"Yeah," Constance was saying. "There's a new girl living with Reed, so we're not rooming together, but—No. She's right here. Okay. Sure." She held out the phone to Sabine. "Whit wants to welcome you to Easton."

Sabine looked surprised, but took the phone. "Hello? Yes. Thanks! It's nice to meet you, as well."

"Omigod, he's so sweet, isn't he?" Constance asked Sabine.

Sabine nodded and smiled as Whit gabbed away. My heart felt warm just watching them. Yep. These two were going to pass Cheyenne's test if it killed me. They were exactly what Billings House needed.

COZY

The day had turned from warm to blazing hot by the time we all headed out for class. Sabine and I walked around the quad together—me in khaki shorts and a T-shirt, her in a layered yellow dress and pink tank that no one else around here could ever pull off—taking the long route so that I could point out the various buildings. Somewhere along the way she took out a tiny blue leather-bound book and pencil and started to jot notes.

"What are you doing?" I asked, amused.

Sabine blushed and hid the notebook against her chest. "I'm awful with directions. If I don't write this down, you'll just have to tell it all to me again tomorrow."

"Right. So this is Hull Hall, but we all call it Hell Hall," I said as Sabine made a quick entry in her book. I lifted my hair off my neck and tied it up in a quick ponytail, trying to cool myself off. "It's where the faculty and deans and the headmaster have their offices."

"I was there this morning," Sabine recalled, tipping her pencil toward the door. "The headmaster had us all meet him there before he brought us to Billings."

"Makes sense," I said, then turned toward the pathway to the library. "Now down here is . . . Josh."

He and Gage were walking toward us from the direction of Ketlar. Josh wore an orange T-shirt that had the words I DON'T KNOW WHAT YOU'RE TALKING ABOUT stamped across the front in brown. Gage wore his usual smirk and a pristine white T-shirt. His gelled hair had gotten about a half an inch taller. He probably thought it looked cool. I thought he looked like he'd just driven through a wind tunnel.

"Josh? Is that a building?" Sabine asked, moving her thick dark hair over her shoulder. I could feel sweat dripping down my back. She looked cool as a winter breeze. "No. It's a guy," I replied with a laugh as Josh and Gage joined us. "Hey."

"Hey," Josh replied.

"New girl," Gage said with a nod in my direction. "How's life in the bowels of America? Your town get that newfangled electricity thing yet?"

Wow. He wasted no time getting right on my case, did he? Picking on me had always been one of Gage's favorite pastimes. So juvenile.

"Dude, she's not new anymore," Josh said.

"I'm new!" Sabine piped up.

Gage turned to her, and an appreciative grin spread across his face. A grin that turned my stomach. "*New* new girl," he said, looking her up and down. "I like."

I wanted to vomit, but Sabine blushed. Ew.

"Ignore him," Josh said, stepping in front of Gage and pushing him away with the back of his hand. "We only hang out with him for charity's sake. Looks good on the college apps. So you must be Reed's newbie. I'm Josh."

"Sabine," she replied. She glanced at his shirt. "I guess I won't ask you for directions."

"You get it! I didn't think anyone would. I was trying to be ironic. Or rebellious. Or something. Since they didn't give me someone to mentor," Josh said. Then he leaned toward Sabine's ear. "Confidentially, I don't know why they asked Reed, either. She knows nothing about anything."

Sabine giggled and looked up at me shyly. Gage's cell phone rang and he answered it, thank God.

"Okay, Hollis. I think your work is done here," I said.

"Please don't offend her. I need her or I'm totally lost," Sabine joked.

"Eh. It takes more than that to offend Reed," Josh said, waving a hand.

"Believe me. I know!" Gage offered, raising his free hand.

"I like your accent. Where're you from?" Josh asked.

"Martinique?" Sabine said it like a question.

"No way! My family used to go down there every winter break! We should talk later. See if we know any of the same people," Josh said.

"Sure," Sabine said shortly.

"Loser! Let's hit it," Gage said, closing his phone. "We've got that new Spanish hottie first period. I want a seat up front so I can work my mojo."

"Dude, hooking up with a teacher is so five years ago," Josh said. But he turned to go. "I'll see you ladies later."

I wasn't sure why he hadn't kissed me, but I was glad he hadn't. I didn't want to go all incoherent and mushy in front of Sabine.

"Listen, Sabine. Gage? You don't want to go there," I told her the moment they were far enough away.

"Why not?" she asked.

"Because he's a man whore and kind of a jerk. Believe me. He is not to be trusted."

"Too bad. But the other one is cute," she said, looking Josh up and down as he jogged away. "They should give us one of those instead of a mentor."

I felt a hot flash of jealousy, but made myself laugh. "Okay, hands off," I said as jokingly as possible.

"I know. I know. He's with Cheyenne. Don't worry. I would never go after another girl's guy," Sabine said, strolling ahead.

It took a good five seconds for my brain to wrap itself around what I'd just heard. Then it felt as if it were slamming into a brick wall.

"He's not with Cheyenne," I corrected her, catching up. "He's with me."

Sabine stared at me for a long moment, her green eyes blank. Then she bit her lip, like she was snagged. "Oh. Really? I thought . . . no. Forget it."

The hot flash of jealousy was now burning brightly over my whole body, the flames fanned by a wave of total uncertainty.

"No. What did you think?" I asked.

Sabine looked around, like she would rather be anywhere but here. Like she wanted to glom on to any of the klatches of students skirting their way around us just to get away from me. This was really starting to get under my skin.

"Sabine. What?" I demanded.

"It's only . . . I saw them when I first arrived this morning. Josh and Cheyenne. Of course I didn't know who they were then, but . . . They were sitting on a bench together and they seemed very . . . cozy. I thought they were a couple."

Okay, Reed. Breathe. You cannot process information without oxygen. And you definitely can't pummel Cheyenne without oxygen, either. Pummeling is serious cardio.

"Are you sure it was them? I mean, you don't really know anybody yet," I pointed out, hopeful.

Sabine seemed to brighten. "Maybe not. Maybe it was another blond girl. There are a *lot* of them here."

That rationale didn't make me feel entirely better. She hadn't exonerated Josh, just put him getting cozy with some other random blonde. Suddenly my stomach was wishing I hadn't insisted on stopping at McDonald's on the way to school. Egg McMuffins and gut-clenching jealousy do not make a good pair.

"Wow. So possessive!" Sabine asked, starting to walk again. "Not that I blame you. I'm sure you're constantly fighting off potential threats with a guy like him."

"What's that supposed to mean?" I snapped defensively. Did she think I wasn't good enough for him?

Sabine's jaw slackened. "Nothing! Just that other girls must be interested. It was a compliment, really."

Guilt permeated my gut and I wanted to smack myself. What was I jumping all over Sabine for? She hadn't done anything wrong. "I'm sorry. I guess I am possessive," I said with a sheepish smile. My insides still felt all warm and gross, but I wasn't going to take it out on her. Cheyenne, however . . .

"No, I'm sorry. I didn't mean to upset you," Sabine told me, touching my arm. "I had no idea."

I cleared my throat and stood up straight. "I'm not upset," I told her. "Josh and I are totally together. Whoever you saw, it wasn't him."

Sabine did a sort of double take as she looked at me. "That was strange."

"What?"

"That look. You just so reminded me of my sister," she told me. "She gets that same venomous look in her eyes when she's talking about guys."

"Venomous? Really? I didn't know I could do venomous," I joked, trying to lighten my own mood. Venomous, huh? Noelle would be so proud.

"Well, you can. Trust me," Sabine said with a grin. "You must love him very much."

"I do," I told her.

I do. More than anything. Which was why I was going to get to the bottom of this Josh and Cheyenne thing. Before my heart spontaneously combusted.

A PIECE OF EASTON

"They're all in there," Vienna told us, leaning toward the gilded mirror in the Billings lobby to check her lip gloss. She touched a fingertip to her bottom lip to remove an invisible imperfection, then fluffed her dark hair. "They look like a bunch of scared little kittens. It's almost cute."

"Kittens," Cheyenne said slyly. "I like that."

I eyed her carefully as she smoothed her already sleek blond do. She was wearing a white blouse with short puffed sleeves and a black pleated mini. Her toenails were red, her fingernails pink, and her skin shone like a Jergens ad. Every inch of her was buffed, waxed, and toned to perfection. But still, I just couldn't see Josh going for her. He was too anti-establishment. Too laid back. Too . . . into me.

"Everyone ready?" Cheyenne asked, looking around at the group of Billings Girls gathered behind her.

"Can I just go on record as saying I don't agree with this?" I put in.

Cheyenne fake-gasped, putting her hand over her mouth. Her sapphire ring glinted in the light from the chandelier overhead. "I'm so shocked! Reed doesn't agree."

I tried to formulate a comeback, but she had already rolled her eyes and strode into the parlor where the new girls were all waiting. My fingers curled in frustration.

"She is in rare form tonight," Rose said, coming up behind me.

"Why are we letting her do this, exactly?" I asked.

"That's why," Tiffany replied as the rest of the Billings girls followed Cheyenne eagerly. She lifted her long-lens camera, focused, and snapped off some rapid-fire shots. "They love this crap. We're outnumbered."

I took a deep breath and lowered my chin. "Let's get this over with."

The couches and chairs were back in their usual places, and Constance, Sabine, Astrid, Missy, Lorna, and Kiki were all gathered in them, forming a U. Cheyenne stood in front of the fireplace with the rest of the girls lined up on either side of her against the wall. Rose, Tiff and I slid into place near the corner, as far away from the action as possible. Like we could remove ourselves from guilt that way.

"Ladies, we've called you here to dispel any uncertainties," Cheyenne began, stepping away from the wall. "The administration may have placed you here, but you do not all belong here."

My heart started to pound. Did she have to be so condescending? Constance and Sabine exchanged a nervous look. I wished I could just go over there and tell them not to worry. But that would have to wait for later.

"Living in Billings House has always been a privilege, not a right," Cheyenne continued, looking down her nose at the girls. "So we, the girls who actually earned the privilege of living here, have decided that you all need to earn that privilege as well. Therefore, we have devised a task for you."

I could see Constance gulp. She knew maybe half of what I had gone through last year, trying to get into Billings. I was sure she was peeing in her pants by now.

"We all think the house could use a little sprucing," Cheyenne continued, lacing her fingers together, arms down, and looking around the immaculate parlor. "We'd like to bring a bit of Easton and its history inside our walls. Your job is to do just that. Find some piece of Easton—something special, something with a story or some significance—and bring it back here to grace our parlor. You have seventy-two hours."

All the new girls exchanged a look of trepidation. Even Missy and Lorna, who had up until now been walking around with their noses in the air like they knew they belonged, had the sense to look ill.

"I'm sorry. You want us to *steal* something?" Sabine asked.

"Is that a problem?" Cheyenne asked, eyebrows raised.

"No. Of course not," Astrid answered for the group, laying her hand atop Sabine's. "I'm sure we've all nicked a few things in our day, haven't we, girls?"

Kiki shrugged. Everyone else was a blank. Why would they ever have to steal anything? Sabine, I wasn't so sure about, but as for the rest? Each of them was worth ten million more than the last.

"Good. All right, then. We'll leave you to it," Cheyenne said brightly. "Three days from now we'll all meet back here, and you can present your offerings to us. And girls? They had better be impressive. This is Billings House. Whatever you bring in here had better be worthy."

She stared Constance down as she said this. Constance shrank back into the couch. Then Cheyenne strode out, followed by Vienna, London, Portia, and the others—all of us—one by one. I tried to shoot my friends a bolstering look as I went by, but they were too busy seeing their lives flash before their eyes to notice.

"Well. That should separate the women from the girls," Cheyenne whispered triumphantly, back in the hall.

"This is so unnecessary," I said, shaking my head.

"God, Reed, what flew up your butt over the summer?" she snapped. "I thought you were cool."

"Likewise," I replied, crossing my arms over my chest.

"Look, I know you miss your little 'friends,'" Cheyenne said with elaborate air quotes. "But I'm in charge now. And I, for one, am not going to let trash take over this house."

I felt like I'd just been slapped. Her unspoken meaning was obvious to the world. She believed that Noelle and Ariana had invited trash in. That *I* was said trash. I wanted to retort, but I was so offended, I lost all ability to think, and Cheyenne took the opportunity to turn on her heel and stride away. The rest of the girls avoided my gaze as my fingers curled into fists. My frustration suffocated me.

In two hours I would come up with the perfect response. And it would already be way too late to use it.

MY GUY

I sat at the end of the pew in morning services the next day, flipping through my assignment notebook, feeling overwhelmed. I already had two papers and two labs due next week, plus a quiz in American history to see how much we had retained from last year. When finals are over, we're supposed to be able to immediately forget all the dates and facts we crammed into our heads to make room for new information. Didn't the teachers know that?

Well, not Mr. Barber, of course. I don't know why I was surprised.

"Everything okay?" Sabine whispered, noticing my maniacal page-flipping.

"Fine. Just readjusting to the insanity," I told her.

"It is a lot, no?" she asked, her eyes wide. "I had no idea. And I still have to choose something to steal for Billings as well," she whispered.

"Don't worry. We'll figure it out," I told her. I wanted to strangle

Cheyenne for putting that tense look on Sabine's face. How was she supposed to know what had history or a story around here? She'd only been here for a day. Even I was having a hard time coming up with ideas.

"And now, I have an exciting announcement to make," Headmaster Cromwell said, effectively snatching our attention. Anyone who had let his or her mind wander during the usual proceedings snapped to. "Next we will be hosting an alumni weekend, which will include a black-tie dinner at the Driscoll Hotel in Easton," he said with a proud smile.

A few people around me groaned. There was nothing exciting about that. The Driscoll Hotel was this castlelike historic landmark in the center of town. It had been built around the same time Easton had opened its doors, ostensibly to host all the wealthy parents and grandparents when they came to town for parents' weekends, graduations, and the like. No Ramadas for that crowd. I had heard it was as gorgeous on the inside as on the out, but had never had the privilege of seeing for myself.

"And each and every one of you will be required to participate in some fashion," the headmaster continued.

"What?" Missy blurted. "He has to be kidding."

Grumbles abounded throughout the chapel. One of the guys across the way pantomimed being hanged from the gallows. Such maturity.

"There will be a decorations committee, a food committee, and an invitations committee, as well as waitstaff and greeters," the headmaster continued, unfazed. "Ms. Ling, the housemother of Bradwell, has graciously volunteered to be the student liaison for this event. You will all see her by the end of the week to volunteer for one of our committees. If you do not, you will be placed wherever you are needed. I strongly suggest you choose for yourselves. Disinterested students might find themselves washing dishes with the Driscoll staff until the wee hours of the morning."

"I don't do dishes," someone near me groused.

"I don't *do* anything," someone else joked.

"You should all see this dinner as an opportunity to present an impeccable image to our esteemed alumni," the headmaster continued, talking over the murmurs and whines. "Let's show them what Easton is all about. Let's show them that this is an institution of which they can be proud."

"And to which they still want to give money," Kiki said under her breath.

"Ms. Ling will keep office hours in Hull Hall each day this week and next between 4 p.m. and 5 p.m. to take your names and preferences," the headmaster continued. "Thank you all for your kind attention. You are dismissed."

"We should volunteer for the waitstaff," Sabine suggested as we got up, the pews around us creaking and cracking as they were relieved of our weight.

"Waitstaff? Why?" I asked. I scanned the crowd for Josh, something that came automatically now that we were back.

"Because then we can circulate all night, meet all the alumni, do a bit of networking," Sabine suggested. "It'll be fun."

I looked at her, impressed. I was sure no one else at this school was hankering to volunteer for the lowly waitstaff. But Sabine was right. I could actually benefit from it. Maybe some wealthy alumni would be so impressed with my ability to handle a tray, he would volunteer to pay for my entire college education on the spot.

Unlikely. But stranger things had happened around here. Many stranger things.

"Okay. Let's do it," I agreed.

"Do what?" Gage asked sidling up next to us with one hand in the pocket of his gray pants. "And can I watch?"

Sabine giggled and blushed. "It's nothing like that."

"Too bad, Martinique," he said, turning around and backing toward the door. "That's a show I wouldn't mind seeing."

Sabine was so red now, she had to hide her face behind her books. This was so not good.

"Sabine, you cannot be crushing on him," I said.

"I'm sorry! I can't help it!" she said, her eyes pleading. "He is *so* beautiful."

Yeah. For a devil spawn.

I sighed and rolled my eyes, dropping it for now. I knew there was no point in trying to talk someone out of an irrational crush on an enigmatic boy. Knew all too well. I could only hope that Gage would show his true colors somehow, before it was too late for Sabine.

"What is that about?" Sabine asked, lifting her chin.

Up ahead, near the chapel doorway, Cheyenne and Astrid talked urgently, their heads bent together. Astrid said something vehemently, and Cheyenne grabbed her wrist, lowering her chin as she gave Astrid some no-nonsense speech. Astrid yanked her arm away, but nodded reluctantly. Then Cheyenne glanced around to check if anyone was watching. The second she saw us, she straightened up and smoothed her skirt, then sent Astrid off into the sun. Astrid cast a look over her shoulder, and I could have sworn it was a guilty one. I had sudden goose bumps all up and down my arms, and not from the cool chapel air. What was going on with them?

"Hi, girls!" Cheyenne greeted us brightly. Way too brightly for the chill that had been rapidly forming between us. "This alumni dinner is going to be so fab. I'm going to volunteer for the food committee. My grandmother's game hen recipe is to die for."

Cheyenne had always had a Martha Stewart streak, but it hadn't reared its ugly head so earnestly since last Christmas and the Billings party she'd thrown. What was up with her?

"Sounds great," I replied. "Something wrong with Astrid?"

"Oh. It's nothing," Cheyenne said, turning toward the quad. "She just misses Barton and Cole. He never came back from France last year, did you know? He fell in love with it during the Barton exchange program and enrolled at his host school."

"Really? That sucks," I said. Though I didn't believe for a second that she and Astrid had been talking about her boyfriend.

"Yeah, but she's known about it for months. It's so past time for her to get over it," Cheyenne said. She quickly checked her gold watch. "Well, got to go. I have to grab some things at the school store before class."

"Wow," I said, stunned by the obviousness of her evasion. What had she and Astrid really been discussing? In her rush Cheyenne bumped right into Ivy Slade and stopped short. The look Ivy gave her could have cut through ten layers of steel. Cheyenne looked at the ground and scurried away. Ivy stood there for a good few seconds, just glaring after the girl.

Okay. *Really* no love lost there.

"I know. Just being around you makes her nervous," Sabine said, reclaiming my attention. "Maybe you should just ask her what's up with her and Josh. I always like the direct approach."

My heart nose-dived into my stomach. I hadn't even thought of that. I had just assumed that Cheyenne was giving Astrid pointers about the Billings test or something. Josh and their supposed canoodling hadn't even entered my mind. Until now.

"Right. Yeah. Maybe," I said, not wanting to dwell on the subject.

"See you in class!" Sabine said with a wave before taking off.

"Yeah. Later."

Was Sabine right? Was Cheyenne really avoiding me—and maybe even fighting me on the Billings stuff—because she had a thing for Josh?

"There's my girl," Josh said in my ear, slipping his warm arm around me from behind. My breath caught and I turned around to face him. He smiled before planting a long, slow kiss on my lips.

When I pulled back, I wanted to ask him. Just ask him what he thought of Cheyenne. Whether they had partaken of some cozy bench bonding that first morning. But I didn't want to be that girl. That girl who asked pathetic searching questions of her boyfriend. That girl who didn't have the confidence to know that he only had eyes for her. That was not me.

"And there's my guy," I replied, putting a little extra emphasis on the *my*.

"You know it," he told me as he laced his fingers through mine.

Exactly. I know it. I just had to make sure that Cheyenne knew it as well.

CAT BURGLARY

"What am I going to do?" Constance wailed, sitting on the rattan throw rug in the center of my room. She was wearing a cute Harvard hoodie Whit had sent her and a pair of gray yoga pants, her red hair twisted into two long braids. "I mean, what do they even want? I know you can't tell me, but . . . can you tell me?"

I barely heard a word she said. I was too busy staring at a new e-mail from Dash, a reply to my last. Part of me had thought I wouldn't hear from him again. That he was maybe just e-mailing me such a short, staid note to let me know that nothing had, in fact, happened over the summer. Yet here he was, e-mailing right back. And this one almost, kind of, sort of referenced that night.

> This Cromwell guy could be exactly what Easton needs.
> Now I *really* wish I could have come back. It might be interesting to see what he does next.

Really wish. So he remembered what he'd said that night. Which means he also might remember what he almost did. I wondered if he was coming to alumni weekend. What if he wanted to talk about what had almost happened? The very idea tied my stomach in knots.

"Reed?"

"What? Sorry."

I closed the e-mail window and turned around in my desk chair. Focus, Reed. Actual drama at hand here. Forget the stuff you're making up in your head.

I recognized in Constance the exact desperation I'd felt last year when Noelle had told me to steal that test for Ariana in the middle of the night. I'd felt trapped. Sick. Frantic to please them and at the same time, pathetic for knowing I'd do anything to please them. But Constance also looked pale. And wan. As if she hadn't eaten all day. Which she probably hadn't. While I had proved to be braver than I had ever thought I was last year, Constance didn't have a brave bone in her body. She was probably making herself sick.

"Constance, they just want you to prove you want to be here," I told her, feeling very wise. At least last year's experiences were being put to some good use. "That's all this is about."

Of course in my case, it was also about Ariana's need to torture me, but there was no point in bringing that up.

"So, can't I just write them a poem or something?" she joked, pulling her knees up under her chin.

"Probably not," I replied.

"Well, what's Sabine getting?" she asked. "Did she tell you?"

"I actually don't know," I said, looking over at Sabine's perfectly made bed. I hadn't seen her since we'd gone to Ms. Ling together to sign up for the alumni dinner that afternoon. She hadn't even been at dinner.

I got up and sat down across from Constance. "I already told you how to break into Hell Hall," I said. "Just take something from one of the professor's offices."

"But it's supposed to have history," Constance said, clutching her knees even tighter. "And I can't go out in the middle of the night by myself and break into a building, Reed. I just can't. Two years ago my doorman caught me going through other people's packages behind his desk and I ended up vomiting on Park Avenue. If I get caught, I'll die. I'll just die."

This was not good. Billings House was no place for a girl with a weak stomach. But it had to be. Constance wanted to be here more than anything. And that should have been the only requirement. Not a penchant for cat burglary. I pressed my lips together and brought my knees to my chin as well, mimicking her pose and trying to think. "Okay, how do we get a piece of Easton history without breaking into a building . . . ?"

"Josh!" Constance exclaimed.

"Josh what?" I asked.

I glanced at my phone as if he were still on the other end of the line. We'd ended our daily 10 p.m. phone call a little while ago. Lots of mushy talk, too embarrassing to repeat.

"Josh has the key to the art cemetery, right?" she whispered, grabbing my hand. "Do you think he'll let us borrow a painting?"

"Um . . . no," I said. "Sorry. I just don't want to suck him into this. He's had enough drama in the past couple of years to last him pretty much forever. And if he got in trouble, I'd hate myself."

"Right." Constance looked dejected. "You're right."

"Okay, but there has to be someone else who can help us. Someone who knows more about this school than we do. Someone who's been here for more than a year."

We looked at each other, the totally obvious hitting us at the exact same moment. "Whit."

Constance's eyes lit up like brights on a Hummer. "Why didn't I think of this before?"

"Call him," I said. "Whit knows everything about this place."

Constance pushed herself up and wiped her sweaty palms on her yoga pants, looking semi-normal for the first time all day. She went to her bag and pulled out her cell phone and a Snickers bar. I laughed to myself as she tore into it. Crisis averted. Whittaker would take care of his girl. Now all I had to do was figure out something for Sabine.

Which I'd be doing right now, if I had any idea where the girl was.

The door to my room opened, and Portia stuck her face, which was covered in a blue mask, inside.

"It's okay. You don't have to knock or anything," I told her flatly.

She rolled her eyes. "Have you seen Shy?"

"Not since dinner," I told her.

Portia groaned and lifted her cell. "Her phone's off, and she's supposed to help me condition!"

I felt a skitter of apprehension. I didn't know what she was conditioning, and I didn't care. All I knew was that both Cheyenne and Sabine were MIA. If Cheyenne was messing with Sabine somehow, I was going to go ballistic on her. Seriously.

"Whit! Hey, it's me!" Constance trilled into her phone.

"Portia, can you excuse us, please?" I said nervously.

The last thing we needed was Portia overhearing this conversation. She narrowed her eyes at the two of us, knowing instinctively something was up, but sighed.

"Whatevs. If you see Shy, I'm in mine."

"Got it." I think.

She banged the door closed and was gone. Now all I had to do for the rest of the night was stare at the clock and wait for Sabine.

QUIT BILLINGS

"Why do you keep looking at your watch?" Josh asked Constance as we inched forward in line at the cafeteria the next afternoon. "Got a hot date?"

Constance's cheeks turned pink, and she almost dumped over her bottled water. "No. Just . . . I have to get to the post office before class, so I need to get some food and scarf it."

"What's the urgency?" Josh asked.

"She's expecting an overnight package," I told him.

"Reed! Shhh!" Constance said, blanching. Her eyes darted around like she was afraid of lurking ghosts. "We can't talk about this outside of—" She looked at Josh and made a choking sound. She really was taking this Billings test seriously.

"Constance, chill. Josh knows what goes on," I told her. He knew because I had, in fact, talked to him about it. Before we were ever even together. Before I knew how seriously some people took it.

"Wait. Are you talking about hazing?" he hissed, his green eyes flashing. "Reed. What the hell?"

Okay. That was a tad vehement. Constance flinched and she looked at me with an apology in her eyes. "I'm just gonna go eat this. Fast," she said, making a swift escape.

"What's up with you?" I admonished Josh. I grabbed a sandwich and an apple and dropped them on my tray. Josh never snapped at me. Ever.

But then, he'd seemed a bit on edge all day. His eyes were still bloodshot like they had been that morning, and his skin was pasty and wan. His gray T-shirt was spattered with blue and red paint along the side, and he had blue paint under his nails. He'd probably been up half the night working on some new creation and had spent the morning half-sleeping through his classes.

"Sorry, it's just I can't believe this crap still goes on," Josh replied. He selected three cookies and a bowl for a to-be-determined sugar cereal, which he ate at almost every meal. "I thought it was all . . ."

He paused and shot me a look, like he wasn't sure if the topic was verboten. I sighed.

"Noelle. I know," I said. "But apparently it wasn't."

It was Cheyenne, too, it seemed. But at least she hadn't been out hazing Sabine last night as I'd feared. Sabine had come in right before lights out, having spent the entire night in the library, catching up. She'd seemed totally fine, if exhausted, and had gone right to bed before we'd had a chance to talk about the Billings test. I had no idea where Cheyenne had been or when she'd gotten home.

"And if Constance wants to be accepted by Billings, she's going to have to play along," I continued. "Luckily she has Walt Whittaker on her side. That's who the package is from."

"Well, maybe she shouldn't want to be accepted by Billings," Josh said bitterly. He jammed down the lever on the Froot Loops dispenser, filling his bowl to the brim. "In fact, maybe both of you should get the hell out of there."

"What?" I blurted.

He snagged a coffee cup and placed his tray down in front of the machine so he could fill it up.

"I'm serious, Reed. What do you really get out of living there?" Josh whispered, looking around in a paranoid way. Only the cafeteria worker, placing grilled cheese under a heat lamp, was in earshot. "Good recommendations? Cool parties? You can get the recs on your own from your teachers, and I can take you to cool parties. You don't have to put up with this crap, you know."

I touched the diamond *B* on my chest, not quite absorbing what he was saying. Everyone wanted to be in Billings. Being in Billings meant being admired. It meant being feared. It meant being the best. You didn't just give that up. Even if it almost killed you.

"I can't transfer out," I told him. "And I don't want Constance or Sabine or any of the other new girls to have to leave either." Except Missy and Lorna, but why bring that up now? "I think it's going to be different this year with them there."

"Not so far," Josh said, picking up his tray. He walked off and I paused, a wave of irritation passing through me. So what if he was overtired? He didn't have to be mean. Part of me didn't even want to go over there and sit with him if he was going to be in that mood.

I was still contemplating this two seconds later when Ivy walked by. She looked me over with her discerning black eyes, shot me a blank stare, and kept walking. What was this girl's deal, exactly? Was she taking mental inventories of my wardrobe? Seeing a perfect opportunity to give Josh a chance to mellow out, I followed her over to the table near the wall where she'd been sitting alone at every meal the past few days.

"Hi," I said, standing across from her as she sat.

She flicked her eyes up at me. "Hello." Dismissive. Cold. I was so unimpressed. I'd dealt with a lot worse.

"I'm Reed Brennan," I told her.

"I know. You're the girl Thomas Pearson was murdered over."

All the air went right out of me.

"What?" I gasped.

"Problem?" Her expression was pure, unadulterated innocence. "It's true, isn't it?"

"I . . ." That was it. That was all I had. How the hell was I supposed to respond to something like that? I had come over here to make small talk, maybe be nice to the girl with no friends, maybe find out if she knew anything about Taylor. From her demeanor around school, I hadn't expected a hug and a warm welcome, but I hadn't expected this either.

"Was there something you wanted?" she asked, lifting her fork. Still totally without guile.

"No," I said. "I think I'm done here."

She stared at me. I stared back, hoping to show her that she didn't bother me. That as rude and bizarre and dark as she seemed, I was not intimidated. I was a Billings Girl. I stared people down, not her.

"If you're done here," she said finally, slowly, like she was talking to someone with a very small IQ, "then you should probably go."

Crap. She was right. What was I going to do, stand here all day?

"Fine," I replied with what little dignity I could scrape together. Then, with her dark eyes fixed blatantly on me, I finally retreated to my table.

BOGARTED

The Easton library was silent, save for the sounds of someone shelving books nearby. So silent, we could all hear Josh's feet bouncing under the table. It happened sometimes. He was a fidgeter.

"Somewhere you need to be?" Cheyenne asked him, smiling in a teasing way.

Don't talk to him. Don't even look at him.

Josh's bouncing stopped. "No. Sorry."

She shot him a knowing look—like they were sharing some inside joke—then got back to her notes. I wanted to pick up my five-pound text and slam her over the head with it. Sabine, at the far end of the table, stared at me like, *See?*

You're just imagining it. That's just Cheyenne. She's a flirt. And maybe she is interested in Josh, but that doesn't mean Josh is interested in her.

But how could she be so obvious right in front of me? Not to mention Trey, who was sitting next to Sabine, slumped so far down in his seat, his ass must have been hanging free. Every now and then he stole a murderous glance in Cheyenne's direction that made me wonder what, exactly, had broken them up. And why on earth he was sitting with us if being near her so clearly made his blood boil.

Josh's feet started to bounce again. Gage let out an annoyed groan.

"Dude. You need to adjust your meds," he said, throwing his pen down. He ran his hands up into his super gelled hair until it stuck straight up on the sides. "Sit the fuck still."

"Dude. There are ladies present," Trey scolded.

"Yeah, kiss my ass, man," Josh added, but stopped bouncing nonetheless.

I touched his forearm with my hand, and he gave me a strained smile.

"You okay?" I asked him.

"Yeah. Just tense about this exam," he replied. He put his pencil down and ran both hands over his face, rubbing hard. When he looked at me again, his skin was blotchy from the pressure. "Maybe I need a break," he whispered. "Distract me."

I smiled happily, feeling needed. "Did I tell you Sabine and I signed up for waitstaff?"

"Perfect," Gage said with a snort. "You can wear your blue collar."

Cheyenne laughed, then covered it up quickly with a cough. I chose to ignore them and glanced at Sabine. Comments like that one had to kill her crush. But she kept stealing adoring glances in his direction. Perhaps there was a translation issue here? I sighed and moved on.

"You should do it too, so we can hang," I told Josh, squeezing his arm.

"Actually, we already signed up for the food committee," Josh said, gripping either end of his pencil with both hands as if he would break it.

"We?" I asked. I had this horrible acidic sensation in my gut.

"Yeah, sorry. I totally bogarted your boy," Cheyenne said, brushing Josh's other arm with her fingertips.

Would it be wrong to systematically break every last one of them off?

I looked at Sabine. She was pretending to concentrate on her reading, but she widened her eyes. She knew exactly what was going on.

"Food committee?" I said to Josh, hoping I didn't sound as shrill to him as I did to me. "Why?"

He shrugged. "We were all talking about it in Lit class, and we just thought it would be cool to all do something as a group."

"We all?" I asked.

"The seniors," Cheyenne said in a superior tone. Like it was just so obvious that they were part of something I was not. "It's our last year. We want to spend as much time as we can together."

"Basically," Josh said.

"Oh." I supposed that made sense. But why hadn't it occurred to him that it might be cool to do something with me? That it would also be our last year together?

"Better get used to it, Reed. There are a lot of senior events," Cheyenne said as she jotted a few notes. "But don't worry about Josh. I'll make sure he doesn't get lonely."

Josh glanced at her, and they both laughed. I felt a flash of anger and jealousy so hot, it could have incinerated the library and everyone in it.

"I'll do waitstaff with you guys," Trey offered.

"Yeah?" I said.

"Yeah. I, for one, have no desire to participate in senior events," he said, glancing derisively at Cheyenne. A look that did not go unnoticed by her. "I'll sign up tomorrow."

"Cool."

"Well that's just fine, Trey," Cheyenne said pertly. "I already have plenty of help."

Her proprietary look at Josh curled my toes. I had to say something. Anything. But what could I say without looking like the psychotically paranoid and jealous girlfriend? How was it that no matter what, Cheyenne always seemed to get the last word?

THE PRESENTATION

I sat in the parlor on the settee on Saturday night, wedged in between Rose and Portia, who could not stop adjusting her hair and elbowing me in the process. Lined up in front of the fireplace were five of our six new Billings residents—or prospective Billings residents, as Cheyenne kept calling them, even though they already did live here—and each had an item on the floor next to her, covered in a sheet or hidden inside a bag.

Constance chewed on her lip and eyed me excitedly. I couldn't muster much more than a smile in return. I was too worried about Sabine, who was conspicuously missing.

"Where *is* she?" Rose asked, sounding nervous.

"I have no idea," I replied.

She had told me several times over the past twenty-four hours that she had this task thing covered, though how, I had no idea. Maybe she had simply decided to bail. Maybe she, like Josh, thought this wasn't worth the effort.

"Well, we said seventy-two hours and it's been seventy-two hours and two minutes," Cheyenne said. "I'd say it's time to begin."

Right then the front door slammed and in ran Sabine, breathless. She held a large black scroll in one hand.

"Is it over?" she asked. Gasped, really. "Did I miss it?"

Everyone looked at Cheyenne. Cheyenne's already straight posture somehow straightened even further. She was enjoying her position of power.

"Don't let it happen again," she said coolly.

Breathing a relieved sigh, Sabine went to take her place at the end of the line next to Astrid, but Cheyenne stopped her.

"No, no. You stand here," she said, placing Sabine between Kiki and Constance.

What was that about? I glanced at Rose, who shrugged. Just Cheyenne being power-hungry Cheyenne. Now that everyone was in place, Tiffany snapped a picture of the whole nervous group.

"Let's begin," our leader said, stepping to the top of the line. "Lorna? What have you brought for us?"

Lorna swallowed hard and looked at Missy, who pursed her lips to urge her on. With a quick throat clearing, she reached into her Neiman Marcus bag and pulled out a small gold placard, bent on one side and scratched up a bit. It read:

DEDICATED TO THE MEMORY OF ROBERT ROBERTSON
CLASS OF 1935

A few of the girls around me snickered. Tiffany's camera flashed.
"You stole Big Bubba's plaque?" Cheyenne asked flatly.

"It's a part of Easton history." Lorna's voice was barely a squeak.

Big Bubba was this monstrous oak tree outside the chapel that had
been dedicated to the memory of some late Easton student named
Robert Roberston. Lorna had stolen the evidence of that dedication.

Cheyenne sniffed. "Well. We're off to an inauspicious start."

Lorna paled as she placed the plaque back in her bag. Her chin
quivered, but she managed not to cry. Suddenly, and much to my
surprise, I felt sorry for her. Lorna had never been much more than
Missy's lackey, really. And maybe her presentation wasn't all that
impressive, but at least she'd tried.

"Missy. Let's see if you can do better," Cheyenne said, stepping up
to Nostril Girl.

"Oh, I can," Missy said simply.

Nice. Way to stick up for your supposed best friend. She reached
into her own bag and pulled out a small leather-bound book. Instantly
my jaw dropped. Rose lifted up from her seat to see better.

"Is that the—"

"The original Easton Academy handbook." Cheyenne was obviously impressed. And well she should be. The original handbook
was kept hermetically sealed in a glass case in the center lobby of the
Easton Library, locked up tight.

"How very black ops of you, Miss," Portia said.

"I know people," Missy replied, pleased with herself. Next to her, Lorna turned green.

"Well. The bar has been set a bit higher." Cheyenne handed the book back to Missy. "Kiki?" she said. "You're next."

Kiki popped her gum, turned around, and picked up a heavy-looking object from the floor. She placed it on the table and removed the blue sheet she had covering it. Every person in the room gasped. It was a small gray, square stone with the date 1858 etched into it, the numbers so worn, they were barely visible. It was the cornerstone from Gwendolyn Hall, the original Easton Academy class building.

"Kiki. What did you do?" I blurted.

"It was no big deal," she said, lifting her shoulders and popping her gum. "All I needed was a crowbar. It just popped right out. Building's crumbling anyway."

"I like this girl," Tiffany said, snapping off a few shots.

"Tiff, maybe you should put that away," Cheyenne said, holding up a hand.

For the first time, Cheyenne looked to be rethinking the sagacity of this little test. Everyone was now eyeing Kiki with a mixture of respect and fear. She stepped back into line and blew a bubble.

"Good point," Tiffany said. She held the camera behind her back.

"Ooookay," Cheyenne said. "Sabine? Not really sure how you're going to top that."

Lifting her chin, Sabine unfurled the scroll and held it up. It was one of the black banners that usually hung between the stained glass windows in the chapel. Embroidered onto it was the year 1984 and the names Susan Llewelyn and Gaylord Whittaker. I couldn't imagine how anyone could get one of those down without a ladder and some help. Impressive.

Cheyenne looked at it for a long moment. "What's this?"

"It is the graduation banner from 1984," Sabine said. "I researched Billings history and found out that Susan Llewelyn is one of our alumnae and she sits on the board of directors. She was the female valedictorian that year. So it's not only Easton history, but Billings history as well."

Rose shot me a look like, *Not bad.* I couldn't have agreed more.

"Who's Gaylord Whittaker?" I asked. "Is he related to—"

"He's Whit's uncle," Constance blurted. "Everyone calls him Guy."

Portia snorted a laugh and fluffed her hair, elbowing me in the cheek.

"Ow," I protested.

She shot me a look like I had inconvenienced her, and turned her knees away from me in a huff.

"All right, moving on," Cheyenne said, stepping past Sabine.

My fingers curled into fists. That was it? No compliments, no nothing? Did Cheyenne not understand how difficult it would be to break into the chapel and get that thing down? Not to mention the research that had gone into it. And Sabine hadn't asked for my help once. If that wasn't Billings material, I don't know what was.

"Constance?" Cheyenne said.

Constance glanced at me before lifting the large Barneys shopping bag off the floor. She hadn't told me what Whittaker was sending her, wanting it to be a surprise. With a smile in my direction, she reached inside and made a yanking motion, but whatever was inside got stuck as she tried for her dramatic reveal. Cheyenne rolled her eyes and clucked her tongue, which only made Constance shakier. Finally, she simply tore the bag down the front and the contents were revealed. Hanging from a wooden hanger was a dark blue jacket with the Easton crest on the pocket, a blue-and-yellow-striped tie, and an ancient blue cap.

"Wow. Nice," Tiffany said from behind me. "That's one of the old Easton uniforms, right?"

"From the early nineteen hundreds," Constance confirmed.

Someone whistled, impressed.

"Doesn't get much more historically significant than that," Rose said.

Constance beamed.

"Yeah. And gee, I wonder how you got it." Cheyenne said, glaring Constance down. Constance backed up a step as if there were actual heat coming off Cheyenne's face.

"Problem?" I said.

"I thought I made it clear that they weren't supposed to have any help," Cheyenne replied, glancing at me. "Did you get this somewhere on campus?" she demanded of Constance.

Don't answer that. Plead the fifth.

"N-no," Constance said.

"So where did you get it?" Cheyenne asked, crossing her arms over her chest. "From your little boyfriend?"

"Cheyenne," I said in a warning tone.

"Whit isn't exactly little," London joked.

Constance's face burned.

"Leave her alone," I said firmly.

"To be fair, Cheyenne, you never actually said they *had* to steal something. Just that you wanted them to bring back a piece of Easton," Rose pointed out. "They just assumed stealing would have to be involved."

As always Rose was there with a very good point. Constance appeared to be buoyed by the backup. She gripped the hanger, her chin lifted.

Cheyenne narrowed her eyes at Rose and her nostrils flared. "That doesn't change the fact that she took the easy way out. And I'm sure her fellow neophytes don't appreciate it."

Actually, none of them had seemed to care until Cheyenne mentioned that they should. Then Missy and Lorna both sniffed in Constance's direction, annoyed. Kiki, however, was eyeing the old Easton cap, probably trying to figure out if she could snag it for herself, and Sabine just looked sympathetic.

Finally, Cheyenne turned and faced Astrid. "And last, but certainly not least?"

Astrid looked around at all of us, hesitating. Nervous? Then she ducked her chin and crouched to the floor. She lifted up an obviously heavy and awkward object, wrapped in a thick blanket, then placed it on the floor in the center of the room. The girls behind me stood so that they could see. Astrid lifted the blanket and stepped back.

Underneath it was an old tarnished copper bell. The kind they used on *Little House on the Prairie* to signal everyone into school.

"OMG," Portia said dramatically.

"How did you get it?" Tiffany asked.

"Now *that* is what I was looking for," Cheyenne said proudly. Astrid's eyes were trained on the floor.

"There's no way," London said, crouching down to see it better. "This can't be the one. It has to be a knockoff."

"A knockoff of a school bell?" Tiffany blurted.

"Uh, you guys?" I said. "What is it?"

"It's the Old Bell," Cheyenne said with a smile. "It hung in the tower in Gwendolyn Hall from 1838 until 1965 when they realized how badly its supports had rotted and they removed it. Ever since, it's sat in the center of the table in the board of directors' chamber."

Trust traditionalist Cheyenne to know every word of the official Easton Academy history.

I looked at Astrid in amazement. I didn't even know where the board of directors' chamber was. How did she know about the bell? How had she gotten in and sneaked out of there with something so huge?

"Damn, girl," London said with a smile. "You have got guts."

"How did you do it?" Tiffany asked.

"Your arms must be *dying*."

The room was suddenly all chatter as everyone gathered around to congratulate Astrid and admire the bell.

"How did you even know about this thing?" I asked. After all, I had never heard of it before.

"I . . . well, I . . . read about it," Astrid said, her face coloring as she glanced at Cheyenne.

Instantly, the truth hit me like an anvil to the head. Cheyenne had helped her. That was what the whispered conference at the chapel had been about. That was why Cheyenne had made sure Astrid was presenting last. Because she knew the bell would make an impressive finale. Here she was getting on Constance's case for seeking help, and she'd guided Astrid right through this thing.

I looked at Cheyenne, and she glanced back, snagged. As I opened my mouth to say something, she clapped her hands for attention.

"Well, well, well. I have to say I'm impressed with some of you," Cheyenne announced as the noise died down. I wanted to say something right then. I did. But I didn't want to embarrass Astrid, whom I actually liked, and whose head was hanging so low right now, she could probably smell her own feet. So I bit my tongue.

"Astrid, Missy, Kiki, good job. You really went above and beyond to impress us. Thank you for that. The rest of you . . ." Cheyenne looked around at Lorna, Constance, and Sabine. "I don't even know what to say. Except nice try."

Constance shrank back toward the wall. Sabine's jaw set. Lorna hugged herself tightly with both arms. I knew it right then. Knew that Cheyenne had decided long before she ever even devised this test, that three people were going to pass and three people were going to fail. Astrid was her friend whose family had taken tea with Prince William on more than one occasion. Missy was a legacy. Kiki was one of the smartest girls in the junior class and the ridiculously wealthy daughter of a computer magnate. They were all perfectly acceptable Billings material. But Lorna was unattractive and a doormat, Constance was sweet and unassuming, and Sabine was, well, my friend. I couldn't think of any other reason why she would be deemed unacceptable. Unless it was just that she was unmaterialistic and kind.

"Cheyenne, come on," I said.

She completely ignored me. "Everyone has their place in the world, girls. I think you three should really start thinking about whether or not you want to keep trying to fit in somewhere you *obviously* don't belong."

Constance looked at me with shining eyes. I wanted to tear Cheyenne's heart out just to show her how she was making these girls feel.

"Tonight you all need to go out and return these things to where they came from," Cheyenne said.

"What?" Astrid blurted.

"I thought you wanted them to spruce up the house," Sabine added.

"Like we can really spruce the house with stolen objects. What kind of idiot do you think I am?" Cheyenne scoffed. "They're going to come looking for these things, and they cannot be found here. I expect each and every one of them to be back where they belong before dawn. Of course for some people, that just means calling the FedEx man," she said, giving Constance a scathing look. "Good luck!" she trilled.

London, Vienna, Portia, and some of the others laughed at the newbies' dumbfounded expressions as they trailed Cheyenne out of the room. Constance turned toward the wall to hide her tears while Lorna ran out the front door. I had never liked that girl, but in that moment I felt for her. For all of them. Even the ones who had won Cheyenne's approval. Now they were faced with sneaking out *again*. With breaking and entering *again*. And in Lorna and Kiki's cases, with replacing things that may have already been damaged beyond repair.

I had never wanted to strangle anyone more than I wanted to strangle Cheyenne at that moment. And with my history, that's really saying something.

THE VOTE

I awoke in the dead of the night when a hand covered my mouth. My heart left my body and I tried to scream, but all that came out was a back-of-the-throat groan. A flashlight flicked on, illuminating Tiffany's face. I stopped struggling. Looked at her, confused. She was wearing an oversized T-shirt and silky pajama pants. She lifted a finger to her lips and pointed at Sabine's bed. I glanced over. Sabine was dead asleep.

"Let's go," Tiffany whispered, releasing me.

"Where?" I rasped.

She tilted her head. Rose and Portia stood at the door. Portia in a floor-length green silk robe, Rose in a pair of DKNY baby doll pajamas. Each held a flickering candle. Color me intrigued. I got up, shoved my feet into my slippers, and walked into the hallway. Tiffany closed the door silently behind us. Portia thrust a candle into my hand and lit it, then handed another to Tiffany. I could hear footsteps downstairs. Murmured voices.

"What's going on?" I asked.

"It's the vote," Rose told me.

The vote? We were really going through with this charade? Really acting like we had any control over who lived here and who didn't? And why the hell didn't I know about it?

"You guys!" someone whispered up the stairs. "Are you waiting for an engraved invitation? Let's go!"

We tiptoed in a line down the staircase and into the foyer. I expected to follow my friends into the parlor, but they turned left instead, away from the darkened gathering space. Toward the back door that had been locked and sealed up for as long as I'd lived there.

"Where are we going?" I whispered.

No one answered. Portia turned another corner, taking us behind the stairs, and I finally understood. The basement. For the first time since I'd lived in Billings, the basement door was open.

"We're going to the boiler room?" I asked. That was, after all, the only thing that was down there. Or so I'd been told.

Someone giggled. Portia shot me a *You're a moron* look over her shoulder and started down the creaky steps, holding her hand behind her candle flame. As I reached the top of the stairs, I could see a half dozen coiffed heads of hair descending before me, the ancient brick walls illuminated by the thin candlelight. There was no telling what lay at the bottom.

Irrationally, my heart started to pound with fear. Or maybe not so irrationally, considering the things I'd been through at the hands of the Billings Girls in the past.

"What's down there?" I whispered over my shoulder to Rose.

"The dungeon," she whispered in my ear.

Joking. But it didn't make me feel better.

Portia was already five steps ahead of me, her robe billowing up behind her as she descended the stairs. Tiff and Rose were waiting behind. It was move now, or move never. I moved.

My knees quaked as I navigated the unfamiliar and uneven stairs. Instantly, the air turned thirty degrees colder. I shivered in my nightshirt, and my candle flame went horizontal. I quickly shielded it as Portia had, and held my breath.

At the bottom of the stairs was a huge slatted wooden door. Open. Beyond that, pitch black. My housemates had formed a circle in the center of what felt like a small frigid chamber. I stubbed my toe on something hard and cursed under my breath. Foot throbbing, I hobbled inside and took my place next to Portia. Directly across from me in the circle were Vienna, London, and Cheyenne. As soon as we were all inside, Tiffany closed the huge door with a creak.

I had never thought until that moment that I was claustrophobic. Turned out maybe I was. I could feel my pulse in every inch of my body. There was an incessant dripping somewhere nearby. Behind me, some sort of box or chair pressed into the back of my calf. I couldn't tell what it was. The darkness was so thick, I couldn't see my feet.

"Welcome, sisters of Billings, to the inner circle," Cheyenne said with pride.

My heart skipped an excited beat.

"Many years ago, our sisters established this tradition, this ritual for the all-important selection of the members of Billings House. Tonight, we continue that tradition," Cheyenne said, her eyes agleam. "Ladies, take your seats."

Everyone around me dropped down. I hesitated a moment—not knowing what was behind me—then did the same. My butt hit the arm of a chair before sliding into a hard seat. I bit my lip to keep from crying out in pain. Cheyenne stepped forward in a beautiful white nightgown, trimmed with intricate scalloping. Her candle illuminated an old-fashioned silver lantern on a table in the center of the circle. Once it was lit, I could see everything in the dim light. All ten faces. All ten chairs. Six easels set up along the wall, each with a black lacquer bowl in front of them. Each with a photo of one of the new girls sitting above. There were shallow bowls dug out of the arms of my chair. In the right bowl, six black marbles. In the left, six white. There was a silver candle holder just behind the bowl on the right side. I followed Portia's lead and placed my candle in it.

"I will call each of your names in turn," Cheyenne said. "When I call your name, please rise from your seat, and place one marble before each of our prospective sisters. Place white if you wish to accept, black if you wish to deny. We'll begin with Portia Ahronian. Portia, please step forward."

I watched her closely from the corner of my eye. She selected three white balls, three black. Shocker. I wonder where those were all headed. Slowly she walked along the line of photos, as if considering carefully. When she was done depositing her votes, she walked back to her chair and sat.

"Thank you, Portia," Cheyenne said. "Reed Brennan?"

Alphabetical, huh? For once, I didn't come in last. I grabbed all my white marbles with a scrape of fingernails against wood, just in case anyone doubted my intentions. It took two seconds to drop them in the bowls, even with my brief hesitation before Missy's picture. I was not going to discriminate, even against her. I was making a point here. Everyone deserved a chance.

I looked Cheyenne in the eye as I walked by her, defiant. She rolled her eyes in return.

The vote went quickly. Everyone, it seemed, had made their decisions before ever entering this room. When it was over, Cheyenne stepped forward and lifted Astrid's bowl. She dumped the marbles out onto the black cloth under the lantern. Ten white balls.

"Astrid Chou has been voted in unanimously."

There were pleased smiles all around. Cheyenne moved to Kiki's bowl. There was one black ball. The rest, white.

"Kiki Rosen has been voted in," Cheyenne announced.

Constance's bowl was next. I held my breath. It took me a moment to count, then count again. Cheyenne sucked in air through her teeth.

"Ooh. Close. Six to four. But Constance Talbot has been denied," she said.

I gripped the arms of my chair. I was not going to freak out. At least not until this archaic bull was over. Lorna's marbles were dumped.

"Lorna Gross . . . denied."

"Missy Thurber has been voted in unanimously."

Shocker.

And then, Sabine. The marbles were dumped. There were five white balls, five black.

"A tie! How exciting," Cheyenne said.

"What happens in a tie?" Rose asked.

"In a tie the most senior member of Billings gets a second vote," Tiffany told her.

"That would be me," Cheyenne said happily.

I stood up. "Wait a minute. How are you the most senior member? I count nine seniors in this room."

"Not senior in school, Reed. Senior in pri," Portia explained flatly. "Cheyenne has pri above everyone else because she's the long leg."

"Long leg?" I asked.

"Longest legacy. My mother, my grandmother, and my aunt were all in Billings," Cheyenne explained with a sniff. "No one else in this room can claim more than two family members."

I don't believe this. I do not believe this.

"And, although it's difficult for me to assume this burden," she continued, all martyrlike, "I'm going to have to say . . ." She turned around and selected a marble from her chair, her perfect blond hair shimmering in the candlelight. She looked right at me with a triumphant smirk as she dropped it among the others. "Deny."

"You are nothing but a power-hungry bitch," I told her, crossing my arms over my chest.

"Reed!" London gasped.

"This is a sacred space, Reed. You'd better watch what you say," Cheyenne told me.

"Sacred? Are you kidding me? All of you just voted on these girls based on one stupid task that Cheyenne pulled out of her ass! And which, by the way, she actually helped Astrid pass. Did you all know that?"

"Excuse me?" Cheyenne asked, hand to chest.

"Don't act all innocent. You were such a bitch to Constance about Whittaker, when we both know you told Astrid all about the bell. I wouldn't be surprised if you even used your connections to get her a key to the boardroom," I told her. "Admit it. You already chose who was getting in before any of us had the chance to vote."

"Is that true, Cheyenne?" Rose asked.

"Of course not," she snapped, eyes on me. "Which is why she has no proof."

"I don't care if anyone else believes it. I know it's true," I said. "It was one totally fixed test." I looked around at the group. "Is that really how you want to choose who you're going to live with for the rest of the year?"

"You just don't get it, Reed. This isn't just about who we're going to live with, it's about who is going to represent us to the world at large," Cheyenne explained condescendingly. "If we want to keep attracting the right people, we have to have the right people in the house at all times. Lorna, Sabine, Constance? They're just not the right people."

"In your opinion," I told her.

"In the opinion of the house, it seems," she pointed out.

I clenched my teeth. "Fine. So you've voted out three people.

What are you going to do now? The headmaster has *placed* them here, Cheyenne. This is nothing but a sham anyway."

"I told you, Reed. There's always something you can do. In this case, no, we can't throw them out of here. But we can make them want to leave," she said.

"What?" I blurted.

"If the three of them decide to bail on their own, then who is the headmaster to stop them? Easton students can request dorm transfers at any time. It's just one of the many privileges our parents pay so dearly for. Well, *our* parents, anyway," she added with a condescending smile.

Very mature. Picking on the scholarship girl. My pulse roared in my ears. No one was contradicting her. No one was telling her how insane this plan was. "So you're going to torture them until they beg to be placed elsewhere," I said, ignoring her personal insult.

"I wouldn't put it in such cruel terms but, basically, yes," she said with a shrug.

"I won't let you do this to them," I said, facing off with her.

Cheyenne chuckled under her breath. "And you're going to stop me how?"

"With my help," Tiffany said, standing up behind me.

Thank God some people around here still had some heart.

"And mine," Rose added, with a bit less gusto. My heart felt all warm inside my frigid body.

"Thanks a lot, Rose," Cheyenne said.

"I just want everyone to get along, Cheyenne," Rose pleaded.

"I mean, do we really need to create drama? Personally, I've had enough."

Cheyenne shot Rose a betrayed look, but recovered quickly. She glanced at the other six members of the house. "Anyone else feel like defecting? Anyone else feel like being responsible for the integrity of Billings going down in flames?"

No one moved.

"Well, then, it seems the sides have officially been drawn." Cheyenne smiled slowly at us, like we were just so amusing. It was all I could do not to smack her in the face. "This should be fun."

PLAYING THE GAME

"I just don't understand how you got the banner down in the first place," I said to Sabine at breakfast the next day, trying to keep the conversation light. Trying not to think about what had gone down in the middle of the night. "You have to tell me how you did it."

"I had help." She toyed with her oatmeal and looked up at me guiltily. "From Gage."

"Gage? Wait. He actually knows the meaning of the word *help*?" I blurted.

"So that's why he missed study group," Josh said.

"He's actually very nice. Once you get to know him," Sabine said earnestly.

Both Josh and Trey cracked up. Sabine dropped her fork and shrank in on herself.

"You guys," I scolded.

"Sorry," Josh said.

"It doesn't matter anyway," Sabine said, staring at her food glumly. "Those girls will never approve of me."

"That's not true," I assured her. "Everyone likes you." Lie. "Cheyenne is just one person. She may seem all-powerful, but she's not."

Not a lie. I've seen all-powerful, and it doesn't look like Cheyenne Martin.

"It didn't feel that way last night," Constance said, leaning her elbows on the table and slumping.

"Not at all," Sabine added.

I sat back in my chair at the usual Billings table, which still felt and probably always *would* feel like Noelle's chair, and blew out a frustrated sigh. These girls were never going to be able to stand up to whatever was coming next if they already felt so defeated by one little test. Next to me, Josh shifted in his seat, avoiding eye contact, most likely because he knew I didn't want to see the *I told you so* in his eyes. Beside him, Trey had decided to ignore the conversation and now concentrated on his bio book. Both Constance and Sabine looked exhausted after spending half the night sneaking stolen objects back into their proper places. I offered to help, but Sabine, Astrid, and Kiki had promised to assist one another and keep me out of it. Constance had gone along as well, swallowing her fear in the name of solidarity. Apparently all had gone well, since none of them had been expelled or arrested or anything. But I knew that every one of them was wondering what Cheyenne was plotting next.

They weren't the only ones.

Cheyenne herself emerged from the lunch line, and the moment she saw us, she fixed her otherwise beautiful face into a sour expression. She strode over with Portia, London, and Vienna on her heels, and cleared her throat.

"Cold coming on?" I asked her.

"Hilarious," she said. "No, it's just that this is the Billings table. Only the most senior Billings residents can sit here."

"Since when?" I asked.

"Since always," she replied.

"I sat here last year and I was a sophomore," I pointed out, knowing that the recollection would sting. Last year Cheyenne had been at the next table, while Noelle and the others had invited me to sit here.

"Yes, well, that was then. You can stay, but your little friends here are going to have to move," she said, flicking her eyes over Constance and Sabine like they were scuff marks on her new Manolos.

"God, Cheyenne. When did you get so bitter?" Trey demanded.

"No one's talking to you, Trey," she replied. "Ladies?"

Constance and Sabine exchanged a glance and both got up. Trey got up with them, slamming his chair back so hard, it smacked into the table behind him.

"No. You guys. You do *not* have to move," I told them.

"It's fine," Constance mumbled, turning around.

She placed her tray on the next table over and yanked out a chair. Sabine took the one next to it, and Trey joined them. I looked at Josh. He no longer had any problem looking at me. He appeared to be sick to his stomach as Cheyenne took the seat next to him and the other girls filled in around us.

"Astrid! Missy! Over here!" Cheyenne shouted loudly, lifting her arm.

Oh, you have got to be kidding me. Astrid and Missy, oblivious to what was going on, came over and took the seats at the end of the table. Constance really looked like she might crumble.

"Cheyenne, there's something I've been wanting to ask you," I said sweetly.

"What's that, Reed?" she asked with false breeziness, playing the game as well as I.

"Do you sleep okay at night or do the horns and the hooked tail get in your way?"

"Oh, Reed. You're so droll," she said, sipping her apple juice. "This is a free country. I can choose who I want to eat breakfast with."

"Well, so can I," I replied, standing and lifting my tray.

"Your prerogative," Cheyenne said with a shrug.

Josh got up as well, but Cheyenne grabbed the arm of his frayed corduroy jacket.

"You can stay if you want, you know," she said, blinking up at him with her big blue eyes.

I was going to scratch those eyes out. Right here and now.

Then Josh smirked and shrugged. "Where Reed goes, so go I."

Cheyenne's face fell. I welled up with pride. I would have said *so there* if it wouldn't have been the most immature thing in the history of spoken language to say. But that didn't stop me from thinking it as I sank into a chair facing her, a perma-smirk on my lips. Josh reached out under the table, took my hand, and gave me a proud squeeze.

So there.

CINDERELLA II

I heard the banging five seconds before my door was flung open. My heart instinctively flew to my throat, but this time, they weren't coming for me. They were coming for Sabine.

"Get up, get up, get up! Get up, get up, get up!"

And this year, they had a chant.

I flung my covers from my legs as Cheyenne, London, Vienna, and Portia barged into my room and over to Sabine's bed. London and Vienna banged pots with the handle side of hairbrushes. Portia had somehow procured a bullhorn. Sabine was already sitting up straight, her eyes wide with confusion, when Cheyenne yanked the girl's flimsy covers off and pulled her up by her wrists. She was wearing nothing but a tiny blue T-shirt and a pair of white underpants. Somehow, she looked very small.

"What is this?" she asked, looking at me over Cheyenne's shoulder.

"You guys, is this really necessary?" I demanded.

They all ignored me. Cheyenne lifted a red-and-white checkered apron over Sabine's head, then forcibly turned her around to tie it. Sabine's long thick hair was still tucked under the shoulder straps and down the back as they shoved her into the hallway.

"At least let her put on some pants!" I shouted.

They left the room without a word or a glance. I groaned and grabbed Sabine's jeans off her desk chair where she'd left them the night before. When I tore into the hallway, every one of my house-mates was already gathered there, and our six new girls were lined up at the wall in their hideous multicolored aprons. Constance's face was dotted with zit cream. Astrid had a sleep line right down the center of her forehead. Missy looked like a football player, there was so much mascara black beneath her eyes. Kiki was asleep standing up. Lorna just looked scared. I walked over to Sabine and handed her the jeans, enduring sour looks from half my supposed friends. Sabine quickly shoved her legs into them and yanked them up.

"All right, girls, this is where the fun begins!" Cheyenne announced. "This is where you prove to us how very much you want to live here. Astrid, Missy, Kiki, you three are on bed duty. Start with my room. And we're talking hospital corners and fluffed pillows, girls! If you cheat, we will know!"

Astrid shook Kiki until her eyes fully opened, and the three of them scurried off toward Cheyenne's room without a peep. Almost as if they had known this was coming. I looked at Rose, who returned my glance with one that said, *I know. What can you do?*

Something. There had to be something.

"The rest of you, bathrooms," Cheyenne said, losing even the false brightness. "We have Clorox and toothbrushes all ready for you. Get to work."

"I'm sorry. We have to clean for you?" Sabine asked.

"No, honey, *I'm* sorry—that you're so slow that you haven't figured it out yet," Cheyenne said, patting Sabine on the shoulder. She leaned forward so that the two of them were practically nose-to-nose. "You want to live here, you have to work for it. That's how it is."

Sabine shot me this betrayed look that made me want to tear my own hair out. "Cheyenne, we have a cleaning service," I said. "Just let them go back to bed."

"Back off, Brennan," Cheyenne snapped. "This doesn't concern you."

"Last I checked, I live here too," I replied. "And I don't see a point in making them scrub bathrooms when the school already pays someone to do it."

"The point is, we all had to do it," Cheyenne said, stepping closer to me. "It's part of becoming an integral member of this house. It's called shared experience."

"That is such a crock," I replied. "Yeah, we all had to do it, but we all hated it. What do you really get out of making more people miserable?"

Cheyenne's face was crimson. "Reed, if you don't like the way we do things, why don't you just—" Suddenly her mouth snapped shut and her eyes darted past my shoulder.

"What is going on here?" Mrs. Lattimer demanded, striding in all clipped and proper. Our housemother was known for her ramrod posture, high collars, and imperious demeanor. Her gray hair was always back in a bun that only accentuated her sharp, birdlike features and beady eyes. "You all heard the headmaster. If you girls are conducting some sort of hazing, I will be forced to report it."

We all closed like a wall in front of the three girls wearing the aprons. Cheyenne and I actually stood next to each other, temporarily united against a shared enemy.

"We're doing our chores, Mrs. Lattimer," Cheyenne said sweetly. "You know we have to get them done before class or this place just becomes a sty."

Mrs. Lattimer eyed her shrewdly. She knew exactly what was going on. We all knew that she knew exactly what was going on. The question was, would Cheyenne's story be good enough for her to pass off to the headmaster if he somehow got wind of the charade?

"Fine," she said finally, clutching the collar of her blouse to her neck. "Cleanliness is, after all, an important virtue in young ladies. I admire your ethic."

"Thank you, Mrs. Lattimer," we chorused, playing our part.

"Well, get back to it, then," she said.

Then she turned and walked down the stairs. We breathed a universal sigh of relief. But it didn't last long. Cheyenne turned to the girls again and barked.

"Why are you still standing here? Get to work!"

As the three of them rushed away, Cheyenne looked up at me and smiled. "Guess that's score one for me!" she sang.

She walked off before I could formulate a response, but I resolved to be ready next time. Maybe Round One had gone to Butt Stick Girl. But she had better be ready for Round Two.

TAKING SIDES

It was 7 a.m. We were all supposed to be at breakfast within the next half hour. As I printed out my paper for English class, I could still hear the girls banging around in bathrooms and opening and closing windows. With each new slam, my muscles coiled a bit tighter. I shoved the paper into my bag and emerged from my room showered, dressed, and ready for battle. Whatever Cheyenne had up her little Lacoste sleeve next, she was going down. Rose, Tiffany, and some of the other girls were gathered just outside my door, looking so tense they could have been awaiting drug-test results.

"They're still working?" I asked.

"They're still working," Tiffany replied grimly.

Cheyenne strode out of her room, clapping her hands. "All right, ladies, in the hall, please!" she shouted.

The six girls came rushing out of various rooms, red, sweaty, exhausted. I knew they were hoping this was it. That they could hit the showers and get ready for their day. But something in Cheyenne's eyes told me this was not the case.

"Before you're done with your morning chores, each of us has a special task for you to complete," Cheyenne said, shooting me a sidelong glance.

What? No, we don't.

"I'd like each of you to select a sister and ask her for a task," Cheyenne said.

No one moved. I saw the other girls exchanging amused glances. They already had chores in mind for these girls. Yet another minor detail Cheyenne had kept from me.

"Chop chop!" Cheyenne snipped. "The longer you wait, the later you'll be for breakfast."

Astrid sighed and stepped from line. "Cheyenne, is there anything I can do for you?" she asked.

"Well, thank you, Astrid. That's so nice of you!" Cheyenne trilled. "Actually, there's this crazy buildup of dust and gunk in the corners of all my desk drawers. It's so nasty. Would you mind cleaning that out for me? Thanks."

She was kidding, right? She was going to make one of her friends late for that? Astrid disappeared into Cheyenne's room, and we all heard the sounds of drawers sliding open, their contents rattling.

"Next?" Cheyenne prompted.

Missy stepped out of line and faced Vienna. "Is there anything I can do for you, Vienna?" she asked politely. I could tell she was proud of herself for her fortitude. For being such a good little plebe.

"I've been meaning to color-coordinate my closet. Get on that, would you?" Vienna asked. Missy nodded and turned away, looking pleased with her cushy assignment. "Oh, and wear gloves. Your fingernails look like you've been digging in manure," Vienna added.

A few people snorted laughs. Missy ducked her head and fled the hall. Every one of my muscles tightened as I willed someone, anyone, to just ask me. Ask me what I want you to do for me. Someone. Anyone.

Kiki cleared her throat and stepped up to me. She pulled her ear buds out of her ears, and I heard angry guitar music screeching from them.

"Reed? Anything I can do for you?" she asked.

She knew. I could tell from the confident way she looked at me. She knew I would not play along.

"Actually, yeah. You can go take a shower and get ready for class," I told her.

Kiki didn't even flinch. She ran for her room.

"Stop! You're not going anywhere!" Cheyenne shouted.

Kiki slammed her door. Enough of a shock for Cheyenne to momentarily lose her will. Quickly, Constance stepped up to Rose.

"Rose? Is there anything you need me to do?" she asked.

Rose glanced at me uncertainly. She bit her lower lip.

You can do this. Screw Cheyenne. End this now.

"No, Constance," Rose said finally. "Nothing I can think of."

My heart expanded to fill my entire chest.

"Rose!" Cheyenne shrieked. "You—"

Sabine stepped over to London. I bit my tongue. Bad choice. Tiffany would have given her a pass, I was sure of it, but London . . .

"Is there anything you need me to do?" Sabine asked.

"Nope," London said with a shrug.

"London!" Vienna and Cheyenne screeched as one. As sounds go, this one was bloodcurdling.

"What? I don't," London said innocently. "I did, but then Rosaline showed up yesterday and practically sterilized the entire room! She even threw out my condoms *and* confiscated my stash. Mother *so* has that woman under her thumb."

This time I did laugh. I couldn't help it. Rosaline was London's parents' cleaning lady. Her mother shipped the woman up to Easton from NYC once every two weeks to clean London's living space, bring her care packages that invariably included diet books she didn't need, and spy on her daughter. This week she'd not only done her job, but had done me a huge favor as well. Cheyenne let out a screech and stormed to her room.

"What? What did I do? Cheyenne!" London scurried after her in her platform sandals. "Cheyenne! Are you mad at me?"

Tiffany patted Rose on the back as the hallway cleared. Constance, Sabine, and Lorna all stood there, however, looking around uncertainly. Didn't they get it yet? They were free.

"You guys. Seriously. Go shower. You're done for the day," I told them.

Then, and only then, did they finally disperse. Guess I had some power around here after all.

THE GAME

"Good morning, tortured souls!" Mr. Winslow strode into our English classroom, all puffed up and loud. "Before we get to our Elizabeth Bowen, let's have your papers!"

I slid the blue folder holding my fifteen-page missive on Edith Wharton out of my bag and stood with the rest of the class. Mr. Winslow cast a cursory glance at the title page of each paper before placing it on his desk. He frowned thoughtfully at some. Others he laughed at, clearly pleased. He was one of the few teachers, perhaps the only teacher, at Easton who could have been considered handsome in any circle. On the young side—which, when it came to Easton faculty, meant pre-forty—he had dark brown hair that actually made it past his earlobes on his more unkempt days, and an easy smile. Plus, by Friday he always gave up on shaving. The dark stubble look really worked for him. But what he really had going for him was that he was human. And nice. Rare qualities in adults around here.

"Ah! Ms. Brennan!" he said as I handed over my offering. "Looking forward to this one." He ticked off my name on his assignment sheet.

I shot him a surprised look. "Oookay."

"What? Anyone who wins Firsts twice in her first year as a transfer student gets a buzz going in the faculty lounge," he said. "Let's hope you live up to the hype."

"Thanks. I think."

I turned around, my heart fluttering with nerves. Should I be psyched that I had a rep for excellence now, or petrified that I'd never live up to it? Somehow I had a feeling it was the latter.

I was about to take my seat again when I noticed that three students had yet to get up. Constance was digging through her bag in a panic. Lorna had removed every last one of her books from her own backpack and was paging through them. Sabine simply sat in her chair, staring stoically forward.

"What's going on?" I whispered to Sabine, sliding back into the seat behind hers.

"My paper's gone," she said.

She didn't move. Just kept staring straight ahead.

"What do you mean, gone?" I asked.

"I printed it out at the library last night and put it in my bag. Now it's gone," she said flatly.

I glanced at Constance, who was still digging, now on the verge of tears. At the front of the room Astrid calmly handed in her own paper. Kiki as well. Missy wasn't in this section, but I had a feeling that if she had been, her paper would have been ready to go.

"Okay," Mr. Winslow said, running his finger down his check-list. "I seem to be missing three papers. Ms. DuLac? Ms. Gross? Ms. Talbot? What have you got for me?"

He looked up with an expectant smile and was greeted by three nauseated stares. His joy disappeared.

"Ladies?" he asked, stepping around his desk.

"It was in my bag this morning, Mr. Winslow," Constance half whimpered. "I swear it was. I can run back right now and print it out again—"

"You know the policy, Constance. If you don't have it in class—"

"You can't give us all zeroes," Lorna said, sounding panicked. "We did the work."

"We can bring them in later," Constance added.

"How fair would it be if the entire class was held to the deadline, but you all were not?" Mr. Winslow asked with a pitying expression. "I'm sorry, but I have to give you zeroes for today. If you like, we can talk about makeup work later."

"But, Mr. Winslow—"

"I'm sorry," he said, making a note on his clipboard. To his credit, he truly did look upset. "There are rules and I have to adhere to them."

As he turned to the board, a couple of kids in the classroom snick-ered. Sabine tore a blank page out of her notebook and crushed it in her first. My heart felt sick. I simply could not believe that Cheyenne had sunk so low. Stealing their papers? This was immature, even for her.

"If this is the game she wants to play, we'll play it," I said under my breath, both to myself and to Sabine. *After all, I'd learned from the best.*

YOUR CHOICE

"I feel so naughty," Tiffany joked, looking down the table in the cafeteria at lunch. She lifted her camera and snapped our picture. "I kind of like it."

Everyone laughed nervously. Even though it was ridiculous to be nervous. But I saw Tiffany's point. The eight of us—myself, Josh, Rose, Tiff, Trey, Constance, Sabine, and Lorna—were the only students in the spacious sunlit room. I had sought each of them out between classes that morning to share my plan, and they had all shown up dutifully. Constance and Lorna had been uncertain at first, but after some wheedling, their resentment of Cheyenne had come through. Lorna, especially, was sick of Missy getting preferential treatment while she was crapped upon left and right. Guess the girl had some personality after all. It seemed like both she and Constance were now ready to take a stand. At least, I hoped they were. The scene we were about to endure would not be for the weakhearted.

Gradually, the lunch crowd started to arrive. I took a bite of my sandwich and waited. My stomach didn't want food right then, but it was going to have to take it anyway. We had to look casual here. That was crucial.

Then Ivy Slade emerged from the lunch line alone, her eyes finding me as they always seemed to lately. She walked right by us, gazing at me as she passed by.

"Hi, Ivy!" Rose said.

My heart caught. She paused. Looked from Rose, to me, then back again. "Rose," she said.

Then she just kept right on walking.

"Okay, what is that girl's deal?" Constance asked, leaning toward the table. "She is creep-adelic!"

"No, she's not. She's totally normal," Rose said.

I glanced across the cafeteria at her. She was still watching me. "I wouldn't say totally normal."

"She's just been through a lot, that's all," Rose said, shaking her head as she took a bite of her food. "We used to be friends," she added morosely.

I was going to ask her more, but that was when Cheyenne, Vienna, and Portia finally emerged from the line, chatting like everything was normal.

"Here we go," I said under my breath.

When Cheyenne looked up, she tripped herself and had to grab a chair for support. Oh, how I wished she'd gone down. It would have made the moment perfect.

"Okay, everyone. Act normal," I told the table.

Cheyenne started the long march over to us in her heels, the fury evident in her very step.

"So you think we're ready for the first game, man?" Trey asked Josh loudly, taking a bite of his roll. "I heard Barton has some sick new talent this year."

"Nah. We're ready," Josh said. He leaned back in his seat, hooking his arm over the back of the chair casually. "Some phenom freshman's not going to take us down."

"*What* do you think you're doing?" Cheyenne demanded, slapping her tray down on the next table so she could cross her arms over her chest. "They do not get to sit here. I thought I made that clear."

She glanced over at Constance, Lorna, and Sabine like they were gnats.

"It's a big cafeteria, Cheyenne," I said coolly. "If our presence bothers you so much, why don't you take that table over by the bathroom? Can't really get farther away from us than that."

"This is our table," Cheyenne said. "Billings always has this table."

"And the next one," I said with a shrug, popping a grape into my mouth. "I guess you could always sit there."

"You are so ridic," Portia said with a laugh. "I mean hilariously ridic."

"No one here is laughing," I replied. "And no one at this table is moving. So you can stand there and hover all period, or you can sit down. Your choice."

Cheyenne stood there. We went back to our lunches. Josh and Trey continued their soccer smack talk. Rose and Tiffany chattered on loudly about alumni weekend and the dinner at the Driscoll. I asked Constance to pass the salt. And yet Cheyenne stood. And stood. And stood. I was growing impressed by her fortitude, actually. But there was no way I was going to give.

"Cheyenne? My feet hurt," Vienna said finally.

"Fine," Cheyenne said through her teeth. She turned around and yanked out the chair behind Constance's, slamming it into her purposely. I bit my tongue. Then, just for the hell of it, she took the chair opposite it, facing me across the two tables. "But this so isn't over," she said.

"Looks over to me!" I replied.

"Freaking priceless," Portia said under her breath as she sat. "I wait three years to sit at that table and now I'm relegged."

"Speak English!" Cheyenne said through her teeth.

"Relegated! God! Take a pill!" Portia replied, annoyed.

I covered my mouth to keep from laughing. Then I saw Kiki, Missy, and Astrid emerge from the line. It was time to put phase two into action. "Kiki! You guys! Over here!" I shouted, standing. "We saved you seats."

They walked over, and Josh and Trey, as prearranged, got up and headed off for one of the Ketlar tables.

"Thanks, guys!" Rose called after them.

Cheyenne's face was perfect. Tiffany, kindred spirit that she was, snapped a shot of Cheyenne for posterity. Kiki slid right into Trey's vacated seat and opened her iced tea. Astrid hesitated for a split second, looking from Cheyenne to me. When her eyes fell on Constance and the others and their hopeful expressions, she did what I hoped. She opted for neophyte solidarity and took Josh's chair.

I knew she was cool. Knew it.

"Thanks anyway," Missy sniffed and joined the others.

No shock there. There was an empty chair at the very far end of the table for her, but no one had actually expected her to take it. I looked down the table and smiled. These were exactly the people I wanted to sit with. These, to me, were true Billings Girls. Round Two had just gone to me.

ONE PERSON

I was still high on triumph when I came around the stacks into the computer section of the library later that day and it all fell to pieces. I stopped in my tracks. Josh and Cheyenne. Josh and Cheyenne sitting with their knees together, facing each other, whispering and laughing and gesturing. Looking, to borrow a word from Sabine, cozy. Cheyenne flipped her blond hair off her face and smiled her Crest-commercial smile, her all-American beauty somehow infinitely more glaring now that it was all up in my boyfriend's face.

"Hello?" I heard myself say.

Josh glanced over his shoulder. His face fell and he pushed backward, away from Cheyenne. She simply smirked as I strode over.

"What's going on?" I asked tersely. I looked at him, not her. I didn't want to have anything to do with her.

"We were just talking about the food committee," Josh said, somehow looking me right in the eye. "We're trying to decide whether to just do passed hors d'oeuvres or have stations at the cocktail hour."

"And I still say stations are too gauche," Cheyenne said to him.

"And I still say hungry guys want carved meat," he replied.

It was flirtatious banter. They were flirtatiously bantering right in front of me.

"You can go now," I said to Cheyenne.

Josh did a double take. "Reed—"

Cheyenne narrowed her eyes at me. "That's fine. I suddenly don't feel like being here anyway," she said. Then she gathered her books and stood. "Call me later, Josh," she said, smiling down at him.

"Yeah. Sure."

It was all I could do not to kick out my foot and trip her as she walked away. I turned and looked down at Josh, my heart pounding.

"What was that?" I demanded.

Josh blew out a sigh. "I know you don't like her right now, but we're working together. I couldn't avoid it."

I dropped my books at the next computer and sat. "Really? Looked a bit chummy for alumni dinner talk."

"It's the library. We were whispering. We had to sit close to each other to be heard." He studied my face quickly. "Wait a minute. You're not, like, jealous of her, are you?" My face must have said it all, because he laughed. "No way. Come on. I thought you were just mad at me because you guys are fighting. Me and Cheyenne? Please."

I hated the way I felt right then. Suspicious and sad and stupid for feeling suspicious and sad. I crossed my arms and stared at the Easton crest in the middle of the computer screen.

"I'm not the only one who's noticed it," I told him flatly.

"Great. So now the Billings Girls are just inventing things to gossip about?" He took my hand and slid closer to me. "Reed, you're it, okay? You're my girlfriend. Cheyenne is . . . not my type."

"Whatever you say," I said noncommittally, unwilling to just accept it. Unwilling to be the girl who just forgets what she knows she saw and believes her man unconditionally.

"God, I wish you would just quit Billings. Being around them is making you paranoid," he said.

"I already told you. I'm not going to quit," I said.

"Why not? You so don't belong there anyway," he said.

"What's that supposed to mean?" I demanded.

He sat up straight, looking momentarily confused. "What? I just think you're so much better than those girls. Smarter, kinder . . . just better."

My shoulders relaxed slightly. "Cheyenne would go nuclear if she heard you say that."

"Just one more reason to ditch the place," Josh said. "I don't want the two of you to be at war."

The two of us. Not me. The two of us. He cared about the two of us.

"Forget it," I said stoically, crossing my arms over my chest. "I'm not going to quit. I'd rather stay there and try to change things."

Josh smiled adorably and reached up to pinch my cheeks. "My little activist," he teased. He kissed my forehead. "I love it."

"And I love when you treat me like I'm some adorable niece," I groused.

Josh looked me in the eye, leaned in, and parted my lips with his, laying a kiss on me that made everything inside me shudder. Made me forget all about Cheyenne and my suspicion. There was no way he could kiss me like that if he liked her, right? It wasn't even possible. When he finally pulled away, I was so out of it, I dropped forward and we almost bumped heads. But he caught my shoulders and held me.

"Better?" he asked.

"Much," I replied, blinking my eyes open.

"Good. I'd better go now. The librarian is staring me down," Josh said, biting his lip. "I'll see you at dinner?"

"I'll be there," I replied.

As he jogged out of the library, I felt myself start to slump. Somehow, I felt let down. Slow. Tired. With a sigh, I turned to my computer and opened my e-mail. There was a brand-new message in my box from Dash. All the hairs on the back of my neck stood on end, and my heart pounded. I opened it quickly, feeling like someone was watching.

> Hey, Reed,
> How's it going with the new girls?
> WB
> Dash

Quickly, I typed a response.

Hi, Dash,

We're on the brink of all-out war, actually. Cheyenne
wants three of the six out and we've sort of squared off. Rose
and Tiff and maybe a few other girls are with me, but I'm
worried I won't be able to stop her.

Advice?

—Reed

I sent the message, then sat back in my chair and, still feeling nervous, glanced over my shoulder. No one was around except for the elderly librarian, who was bent over a book, as always. The computer gave a low beep, and my heart caught. Apparently Dash was online, because he'd written right back. Hand shaking, I clicked open his message.

Reed,

Do not be nervous. If there was one person at Easton
I could always count on to be on the right side of things, it
was you. Do not let Cheyenne make you feel otherwise. You
have the high road. I'll be thinking of you, sending good
vibes your way.

—Dash

I read the e-mail twice. Then a third time. Something stirred inside my chest. For the first time all day, I felt certain. And proud. I couldn't believe that was how Dash McCafferty saw me. And he said he was thinking of me. Thinking of *me* . . . A blush crept across my cheeks. Dash McCafferty was sitting in his dorm room at his Ivy League school thinking about little Reed Brennan.

A loud bang somewhere in the stacks startled me, and I quickly shut the window, scared half to death. Instantly I thought of Noelle. Imagined how furious she would be if she knew that Dash and I were in contact. If she knew that his e-mails made me blush. Which, of course, made me think of Josh. What the hell was I doing? I'd just accused him of flirting with Cheyenne, yet here I was doing almost the exact same thing with Dash. What was the matter with me? Overwhelmed by guilt, I deleted Dash's e-mail and fled.

WHISPERS

Study break at Billings House that night consisted of Chicago-style pizza that Tiffany's friends from home had FedExed to her and she'd heated up in the illegal microwave in her room, along with several bottles of champagne, or "Dommy P" as Portia called it, which her twenty-three-year-old oil-magnate boyfriend had sent to celebrate the start of her senior year. Everything was calm, considering that war had been declared. I knew better than to trust the lull, but I wanted to. I wanted just five seconds without drama. So I grabbed a slice and joined the others in the parlor, where they were watching *Batman Begins* for the twenty-fifth time—or, more accurately, just pausing it on particularly hot Christian Bale moments. I was just starting to enjoy myself when I realized Sabine wasn't there. Cheyenne and Vienna weren't there either, but that was not a point of concern.

"Hey. Have you seen Sabine?" I asked Rose as she tipped her champagne flute to her lips.

"I think she's upstairs," she said. "Oooh! Shirtless!" she shouted, waving her hand at the screen. "Someone pause!"

I dropped my pizza crust on the china plate donated by some elderly Billings alumnae and headed upstairs. Sabine had been almost silent all day long. I hoped she wasn't planning on asking for a transfer. Cheyenne would be unbearable after a victory like that. And besides, if there was one thing I knew about Billings, it was that sticking it out was the best policy. Getting through all Noelle's tests and pranks had been a serious source of pride for me. I wouldn't be the person I am now without it. And I wanted that for Sabine. I wanted her to be the person who was able to stand up to Cheyenne.

On a selfish note, I didn't want her to leave me. I was starting to get used to having actual friends around.

I pushed open the door to our room, but it was empty. Her desk light was on, but there was no sign of her. Then I heard voices down the hall. Intense, low tones. Coming from Cheyenne's room. I felt the same skitter of apprehension I had always felt when Noelle and Ariana were talking alone. I held my breath and tiptoed toward them.

Just outside Cheyenne's doorway, I paused and listened.

"No. I'll get it. I'll do it," someone said in a low tone.

I wasn't sure who was talking, but it was so urgent, it made all the hairs on my arms stand on end. Get what? Do what? Then someone else replied so quietly, I couldn't make out the words. Dammit. Had to go for plan B. I turned around and shoved open the door, about to say something snarky. But instead, I froze. It wasn't Vienna that Cheyenne was talking to. It was Sabine.

"What's going on?" I asked.

There were clothes laid out on the bed, high-heeled wedges and boots on the floor.

"Nothing." Sabine was calm as a warm bath.

"I'll be here," Cheyenne said to her in a meaningful way.

Sabine nodded and started past me, her eyes down. I followed her into the hallway. "Where're you going?"

"Cheyenne needs a book from the library," Sabine said. Her eyes were oddly bright. "I'm just going to run and get it."

I looked out the plate glass window at the end of the hallway. It was pitch black and raindrops battered the panes like they were desperate to get inside.

"Now?" I asked. I looked at Cheyenne, who sat primly on her bed, her knees together and her hands folded. "Let her get it herself."

"Reed, it's okay," Sabine said through her teeth. She stepped closer to me and whispered. "I think she's actually starting to accept me. She just gave me all this advice about Gage. She's going to help me with him, but I have to keep playing her game."

"Help you with him?" I was flabbergasted. From the way Gage had been acting, all Sabine had to do was put his hand on her butt and he was hers. For a day, anyway, which was probably about as long as his attention span would stretch for anyone. Other than Ivy, if those rumors were true.

"Reed, I know you don't like him, but I do. I can't help it." Sabine sounded desperate. "Just let me go."

I looked into her eyes and saw that she meant business. Cheyenne had played the unrequited love card, and she had her.

"You don't have to do this, you know," I told her. Even though I knew it would have no effect.

"I know," she replied.

Then she shot me a look of thanks before she headed out. I stepped back into the doorway of Cheyenne's room. She was folding clothes now, and she paused. We stared at each other across the wide expanse of her single. Her lips were twisted into a superior smirk.

"So. You're going to 'help' her, huh?" I asked.

She heaved a dramatic sigh. "I am so over your attitude."

"Why are you doing it, Cheyenne?" I demanded.

"I can see you're not going to go away until I humor you, so fine," she said, folding a sweater over her arm. "The girl has a crush, and you know I'm a sucker for love. Besides, I happen to know what Gage likes. Intimately."

Good Lord. Was there anyone those two hadn't been with?

"So, what? You're going to dress her up like you and send her to the big bad wolf?" I asked.

"Why do you think everything I do has malicious intent?" Cheyenne asked. "Maybe I'm starting to see some potential in Sabine. Maybe I want to see her happy."

Yeah, right. And maybe I'm America's Next Top Model.

"You can go now," she said with a sweet smile.

I eyed her for a long moment, trying to see her angle. Trying to get into her devious brain, think three steps ahead, and find the loophole, but there was nothing. My brain just didn't work that way. There was nothing left for me to do but walk away and wait.

THE FIRST TIME

I waited behind the huge maple tree outside Ketlar the next morning until I saw Mr. Cross, the elderly Ketlar advisor, amble out the back door, whistling to himself. A couple of guys followed, and as soon as the door was closed, I slipped inside and ran up the stairs to the fourth floor. Josh's floor.

I needed to see him. Now. Needed to kiss him and make sure everything between us was okay. Ever since I'd seen him with Cheyenne yesterday, I had felt this queasy uncertainty inside my chest. Couple that with the guilt over the Dash e-mails, and my legs went shaky. I couldn't walk around Easton all queasy and shaky like this all year. It was not good for my nerves. I needed to be with Josh. Really be with him. Look him in the eye and tell him how I felt. Really felt. For the first time. That would make everything okay.

Trey was just coming out of their room as I approached, breathless. He took one look at me and smiled knowingly.

"He's all yours," he said, holding the door.

We all pretty much lived to break the rules around here. Like the one that would prevent me from being in a guy's room. Even straight-as-an-arrow Trey.

"Thanks," I whispered. I slipped inside and shut the door. Josh looked up at me, surprised. Not as surprised as me, however. He was standing near the window, still wet from the shower, wearing nothing but a towel around his waist. His smooth chest was perfect and glistening, and the definition in his arms was far more distinct than I remembered. My mouth went completely dry.

"What are you doing here?" he asked with a smile.

"I . . ."

Wait, what was I doing here again?

Didn't matter. Because two seconds later his hands were in my hair and his lips were over mine and we were kissing and touching and stumbling and falling and things got very heavy, very fast.

"Wait!" I blurted, pulling away from him on his unmade bed.

He let go of me, his eyes at half mast. "What? Did I . . . Are you . . . What?"

My heart was pounding so hard, I thought it might bruise itself. I stood up, leaving my half-naked boyfriend confused, and probably very aroused, on his bed. Deep breath, Reed. Deep breath.

"I didn't come here for this," I said firmly, standing in the center of his room.

Josh sat up straight, legs over the side of the bed, and placed his arms over his lap in an awkward way. He looked up at me and tried to concentrate. "Okay. Why did you come here?"

I gazed into his clear green eyes. His chest heaved as he got his breathing under control. But he was focused on me. On my face. Waiting patiently. I could do this. I could. Because I meant it. And because I trusted him. And it didn't matter what happened next. I just wanted him to know. My fists uncurled. I breathed in. And when I let the air out again, I said it.

"Josh, I love you."

His whole face lit up. He stood, looking into my eyes with this wondrous expression, like I'd just given him the most incredible gift he'd ever received. Then he kissed me, slowly this time. Slowly, softly, deeply, and when he pulled back, he was clinging to me like he'd never let go.

"I love you, too."

Relief. Even though I had known he would say it—that he'd wanted to say it all those months ago when I'd almost left Easton for good—part of me had been afraid. That he'd changed his mind. That he'd never felt it in the first place. But he did. He still did.

"You have no idea how long I've been biting my tongue to keep from saying that to you," he half whispered. "After that day when you stopped me—"

"I know. I'm sorry," I told him. "But it doesn't matter anymore. Now you can say it as much as you want."

Josh took a step back, eyebrows raised adorably. "Really? You mean I can say I love you? I love you, I love you, I love you?"

I cracked up laughing.

"I like the way it sounds, just coming off my tongue," he said, gesturing with his hands. He yanked a T-shirt out of the closet and pulled it on over his head. "I love you. I love you, I love you, I love you. Huh. Cool."

"Okay. Let's not wear it out on the first day," I said, so giddy inside, it was almost too much.

"Yeah, yeah. You and your rules."

He took a pair of boxer briefs out of his drawer and pulled them on under the towel, then did the same with a pair of cords, and shed the towel completely. Then he jammed his feet into his suede sneakers and grabbed his messenger bag.

"Breakfast, my love?" he asked, opening the door for me.

"Why, yes, my love," I joked back.

He kissed me again on my way through the door and we swung our entwined fingers between us as we walked to the cafeteria. It no longer mattered whether Cheyenne wanted him or not. Josh was mine. No one was ever going to come between us.

HAPPINESS

"Where's Sabine?" Trey asked me at breakfast.

Her chair, across from mine, was conspicuously empty. The sun pouring through the skylight overhead sent a bright shaft of light right across it like it were trying to spotlight the fact that she wasn't there.

"She was still in the shower when I left," I told him.

Josh took my hand under the table and squeezed. My heart felt like it was playing on the uneven bars. He leaned in to whisper in my ear.

"Hey, have I told you I love you?"

Shivers everywhere. "Yeah, I think I've heard that somewhere before."

Happiness. This was what happiness felt like.

Gage strolled by with his tray, his aviator sunglasses covering his eyes, and the sight of him didn't even irritate me. Happiness. Then Cheyenne pushed herself up from the next table and slithered over to him. Didn't care. Not one bit. Happiness.

"Ga-age! I have a surprise for you!" Cheyenne sang.

He looked her up and down. "Been there, done that."

She managed to laugh as if she wasn't offended. "Not me. Just stand there for one . . . more . . . second."

As if on cue, Sabine emerged from the breakfast line, carrying a tray full of food. But she didn't look anything like the island girl I knew. She looked like a New England tartlet. Plaid mini. Bare knees. High-heeled boots. Tight, white, button-front shirt. Sleek, slicked-back ponytail. As she came around the first table, her feet wobbled slightly, unaccustomed as she was to heels, but she recovered nicely. Gage didn't seem to notice at all, of course. His tongue was practically hanging out.

So this was Cheyenne's plan to help Sabine. Turn her into a Pussycat Doll and let her loose on society. I loathed her.

"Martinique goes naughty Catholic schoolgirl," Gage said in awe. "I like."

Sabine smirked—a look that was an eerie mirror of one of Cheyenne's favorite expressions—and opened her mouth to say something Cheyenne had undoubtedly coached her to say. And then, suddenly, it all went wrong.

Her already unsteady foot hit a puddle of water and slipped out from under her. Her eyes went wide. There was an ever-so-brief moment when I thought she might have recovered, but it was only an illusion. Sabine flew off her feet and slammed into the ground, butt and back first. White underwear for all the world to see. Her tray went airborne and rained cereal and eggs all over her pristine white shirt. Orange juice splashed in her face. For a long moment, no one moved.

And then, laughter.

Gage doubled over. Cheyenne convulsed. The entire cafeteria filled with cackling cacophony. As I stood to help Sabine, she sat up and looked around, her face filling with anguish. She yanked her skirt down over her underwear, clinging to the hem. I had never seen anyone look so small.

Out of the corner of my eye I saw Cheyenne draw her hand across Portia's palm. It was an infinitesimal movement. If I'd blinked, I would have missed it. But I didn't. I saw it. And I knew. She had spilled that water in the center aisle. She had lent Sabine, who owned only flat sandals and flip-flops, her highest heels. She had orchestrated it all. And my rage was beyond compare.

"You did this," I said to her, shaking.

"Oh, get off your high horse already, Reed," Cheyenne said. "The thin air up there is affecting your brain."

Sabine finally got up off the floor and ran, awkwardly in her heels, for the door.

"You are so going to regret the fact that you ever met me," I told her.

"You're forgetting something, Reed," she replied. "You started this. You drew the line that night at the vote. Whatever happens next, it's all your fault."

I wanted to smack her in the face. Wanted to take her feet out from under her and show her how it felt. But this was not the place, and I had no time. I had to go after Sabine.

"This is not over, Cheyenne," I promised her. "Not even close."

PARALYZED

Sabine spent the entire day in the infirmary. When I went to check on her, they wouldn't even let me see her. Said she wanted to be alone. After dinner, which she had skipped, she had come back to the room, grabbed her books, and left again, ignoring my attempts to talk to her. Just ducked her head and disappeared.

Now it was 10:17 and still, she wasn't back. The library had closed seventeen minutes ago. Where the hell was she?

Please, just don't let her drop out. Don't let her give Cheyenne the satisfaction.

I took a deep breath and glanced at my cell phone. Josh was also MIA. I hated being one of those girls who sat around waiting for her phone to ring, but that's what I was doing. I needed to talk to him. Needed to vent about what had happened and hear his levelheaded take on where Sabine might be. Josh always called me at ten. Every night before bed. But tonight, nothing. Even after the most perfect morning of our relationship. Those kisses that still gave me warm shivers every time I thought about them. Nothing.

The clock clicked over to 10:18. Something had to be wrong. I was just reaching for the phone when the door to my room burst open.

"Reed!"

"Oh my God! You scared the crap out of me!" I said, laughing. I turned to look at Constance and Sabine, and even though I was happy to see that Sabine was all right, my heart instantly dropped to the floor. They looked as if they'd both just witnessed a car wreck. "What's wrong?"

They glanced at each other with trepidation. My heart thumped extra hard.

"What is it?" I asked, my throat closing.

"It's Josh," Constance was so apologetic, I wondered for a second if she'd done something to him somehow.

"What about Josh?" I was on my feet.

"You have to come," Sabine said, reaching for my arm. "Just come."

Fear expanded inside me, filling up my every pore. I couldn't move. "Come where?"

"Reed—"

"I'm not going anywhere until you tell me what's going on," I said firmly. "Tell me. Right now."

Another grim look passed between them. "We saw him, Reed," Sabine said finally. "With Cheyenne."

DIGNITY

I ran.

I ran so fast, my lungs burned and my vision blurred. I ran so fast, I couldn't hear a thing save for the wind in my ears. I ran so fast, I tripped over one of the lights lining the pathway and was sent sprawling, tearing up my knee, my hand, my cheek, then got up and just kept running.

He loves me. This isn't happening. He loves me. He loves me.

Sabine was at my side when I arrived at the tall windows of the art cemetery. Constance was miles behind.

"Reed, take a breath first," Sabine said. "Calm down."

"No. No!" I shouted.

I didn't care if anyone heard. Didn't care if I got expelled. I just wanted to see. I needed to see. I crept through the bushes to the windowpane. The blinds were cracked so that one could easily see through the slats. I closed my eyes. Said a prayer. Gripped the cold stone cornice with my fingertips. And looked.

Something frigid and slimy slithered down my spine. The edges of my vision went hazy and gray. Inside the warm glow of the art cemetery, our sanctuary, the place Josh and I had shared many stolen moments, stolen kisses, stolen whispers, he was now lying back on the love seat as Cheyenne climbed on top of him.

I felt the vomit coming just in time to turn my head away from Sabine. I retched into the mulch at my feet. Strained tears streamed from the corners of my eyes, down my nose, and across my lips.

But he loves me. He said that he loves m—

"Reed, I am so so sorry," Sabine said.

"No," I heard myself say. "No."

I drew the back of my hand across my mouth. Looked again. Josh reached up and cupped the side of Cheyenne's neck lovingly, his eyes worshipping. He let his hand slide down and nudge her blouse off her shoulder as she ever-so-slowly unbuttoned it.

"No!"

That was it. No more. I turned and shoved Sabine out of the way. Ripped open the door to Mitchell Hall. I was about to bang on the door to the art cemetery when I saw that it wasn't even all the way closed. With both hands, I shoved it open. It banged against the wall. A painting crashed to the floor. Cheyenne jumped up with a gasp and righted her shirt, covering her lacy, barely-there bra. Her skirt was on the floor. Her thong and perfectly tanned ass exposed.

"Reed," Josh said. "Reed, what are you—"

"Shut up," I said, tears streaming from my eyes. "I don't want to talk to you. I don't even want to look at you!" I wiped my face quickly and held my breath, not wanting to give Cheyenne the satisfaction of seeing me this way.

Josh pushed himself up onto his elbows and stared at me. His T-shirt—the very T-shirt he'd put on this morning right in front of me—was pushed all the way up to his pecs. His cords were unbuttoned, unzipped. I felt bile rise in my throat again and swallowed it back. Why had he not jumped up like Cheyenne? Why was he not begging for forgiveness right now? Was every single minute of that morning a lie? Did I really mean that little to him?

"Calm down, Reed," Cheyenne said huffily, doing up her buttons. "I know this is hard for you, but at least try to retain some dignity."

And that was when I finally did it. That was when the tenuous rope inside me finally snapped and I slapped Cheyenne as hard as I could, right across her pretty little face.

WILLING PARTICIPANT

"You pathetic, two-faced little whore!" I shouted, storming into Billings House with Sabine and Constance right on my heels. Cheyenne raced ahead of me and jogged up the stairs in her high heels.

"Leave me alone, you psycho!" she shouted back at me.

I took the stairs two at a time and followed her to her room. All the doors in the hallway were already open. Girls crowded into doors in their pajamas, watching as we tore by.

"Reed! What's going on?" Rose asked.

Like I could answer that right now. I had a blonde to disembowel.

He'd said he loved me. He'd said he loved me.

But she'd just taken it all away.

Cheyenne tried to slam her door in my face, but I flattened my hand against it and pushed my way in.

"Get out!" she shouted at me, backing toward the window.

"Not until you admit what a fraud you are," I told her.

"You're crazy, Reed. You've finally snapped," Cheyenne ranted, laughing nervously.

"Oh, I'm crazy. I'm crazy?" I blurted. "You walk around here for days blabbering on about Billings and integrity and image and sisterhood and bonds that will last a lifetime and meanwhile you're spending every single free second you have seducing my boyfriend!"

There was a general gasp and twitter behind me. I turned to look. Every single one of our housemates was either gathered near the door or out in the hall.

"That's right, girls! Your fine, upstanding leader was just straddling my boyfriend in the art cemetery," I said, knowing they would all find out through the rumor mill anyway. "And yet she's the one walking around telling all of us who's good enough to be in Billings. Who has the right qualities. This backstabbing *slut* is passing judgment on everyone else!"

"It wasn't just me, Reed. I didn't throw myself at him," Cheyenne said. "You saw him. He was a willing participant. He even invited me there."

My vision blackened over. I honestly felt as if I might faint. When I whirled on her again, I had to grab her dresser to keep the dizziness at bay. It was one thing if Cheyenne had gone to him. If she'd known he'd be there like he was most nights and had walked in wearing her sexy little outfit all toned and blond and sexpotted out. I would still never forgive him, but it would somehow make it better to put the fault squarely on her.

"I don't believe you. I've seen you. I've seen the way you're all over him all the time. This was all you."

"Oh, yeah? Here!" Cheyenne reached into her Kate Spade and pulled out her cell, tossing it at me. "Check the first text message."

She was bluffing. She had to be bluffing. I opened the text window and my vision blurred again. There was Josh's cell number across the top of the screen, clear as day. The message read:

> cant wait anymore. NEED u. now. 2nite. meet me. art cemetery. after cmte meeting.

Every ounce of rage I had within me exploded at that moment. I reached back and hurled her phone at the wall, shattering it into a million pieces, one of which nicked Cheyenne right in the face. Cheyenne yelped and cupped her chin.

Mrs. Lattimer chose that moment to show up.

"Girls!" she shouted. "That is enough!"

The shock, the horror, the disgust, was evident in her eyes as she took in the scene. Cheyenne, still haphazardly dressed. The pieces of the phone all over the floor. The mask of purple fury that I knew was covering my face. Her mouth formed a thin line of determination. I had never seen her look so grim.

"To your room, Miss Brennan. Now."

REINFORCEMENTS

"Who the hell does she think she is? She thinks she can just do whatever she wants? *Have* whatever she wants?" I ranted, whisper-shouting myself hoarse as I paced in front of Sabine. She sat in the center of her bed, knees together, watching me as I walked back and forth. Only her eyes moved. It was as if she was afraid to shift position lest I pounce. Not that I could blame her. I was rabidly out of control. "*Who*ever she wants?"

My voice cracked and I stopped pacing, covering my mouth with my hand as the images came rushing back to me. Josh's hand on her bare skin. That adoring look in his eyes that used to be reserved for me. He'd looked at Cheyenne the exact same way he'd looked at me this morning when I'd told him I loved him. The *exact* same way.

My other hand went to my stomach. How could he? How could he do this to me? Was this the reason he'd wanted me to quit Billings so badly? To keep me and his other woman apart? Less chance of me finding out about her if we weren't living together, I suppose. And, oh my God. That night. That night Cheyenne had been out so late and I thought she'd been with Sabine . . . Had she been with Josh then, too? He'd been exhausted and cross and impatient the next day. Had this been going on this whole week? Had they been lying to me from day one? I couldn't believe Josh could be that manipulative. That cunning. No. Not Josh. Not possible.

But then, I would have never thought this was possible. Never in a million years.

"She is out of control," Sabine agreed. "You used to be friends, no? Even if you have had problems this year, it's no excuse."

I took a deep breath to quell the nausea. Wiped a stray tear from under my eye.

"'Out of control' is an understatement," I blurted. "You know she's been trying to force you, Constance, and Lorna out of here since that first day, right? She doesn't care if you quit Billings or get expelled. Whichever happens first is fine by her."

Sabine's jaw dropped. "Expelled? She wants us expelled? My father would murder me!"

"She doesn't care. As long as you're not living here," I muttered.

"But . . . but I haven't done a thing to deserve it," Sabine said, standing. "I've done everything she asked. Running her errands . . . cleaning her room . . . stealing things and putting them back. I've done nothing wrong. She is the one who's manipulating everyone. It's not fair!"

I leaned into my desk and stared out the window at the lights on the quad. "You're right. Cheyenne's the one who should get expelled, after everything she's done."

My words hung in the air between us. Sabine was perfectly silent. Perfectly still. My heart started to pound anew. Cheyenne. Expelled. Cheyenne. Expelled.

This was supposed to be a perfect year. New and free of drama. And it would have been, if not for her. She had ruined it all. Ruined Billings. Ruined Josh. Ruined everything. I looked at Sabine. Her eyes were wide. We were thinking the same thing. My skin tingled.

"What if she did get expelled?" I said slowly.

"It would be over then, no?" Sabine said tentatively.

"God, can you even imagine how peaceful it would be here without her?" I said, looking around our room. "Without her torturing you guys? Without her stomping and shouting and ordering people around?"

"We could just be students again," Sabine said, sounding wistful. "We could be normal."

She was right. If Cheyenne were gone, the newbies would be spared any more stress. They wouldn't have to go through all the crap I'd gone through last year. I was certain that without Cheyenne leading the pack, the hazing would end. Portia was too self-involved to be bothered, and Vienna and London would rather be primping and partying than plotting. Without Cheyenne, Billings would be free.

I would just love to see her face if she got expelled. Would love to show her once and for all that she couldn't mess with me. That I wasn't going to just let her get away with stabbing me in the back.

I couldn't believe I was seriously considering this. Couldn't believe I actually had it in me. But then I thought of Josh again. His face. His hands. His eyes. And I knew that I could do it. I was more than capable.

"Do you think we could do it?" I said quietly.

Sabine bit her lip. "I wouldn't even know where to begin."

I sat down shakily on my desk chair. My computer screen was dark, but just looking at it gave me an idea. God, if only Noelle were here. She would know exactly how to exact revenge on Cheyenne, and exactly what strings to pull to get the job done. But I didn't even have a clue where she was, how to get in contact with her. She had long since changed all her numbers and e-mails, as if she wanted to cut off everyone completely. Cut me out of her life. But I had a feeling she would want to hear about this. Would want to help. She, after all, cared about Billings more than anyone. And one of her worst fears had been finding out what would happen if Cheyenne took over.

I stared at the computer. I knew someone who might know how to find her. Someone I'd been "talking" to nearly every day. Maybe it was finally time to broach the subject I had been avoiding for so long. Could I do it? And if I did and he helped me find her, would she be there for me?

I hit the space bar, bringing the screen to life.

"What are you doing?" Sabine asked.

I typed in Dash's e-mail. "Calling in reinforcements."

I composed a quick message, but the second I hit the send button, I wanted to call the e-mail back. My whole chest filled with dread.

What was I thinking? I was not Noelle. I had made that abundantly clear over the past few weeks. I couldn't get someone expelled. Not even Cheyenne. I wasn't a schemer. I didn't have it in me. This was not me.

And on top of all that, what if Dash didn't write me back? We never mentioned Noelle or Josh in our e-mails. What if bringing her up now somehow tarnished our banter? Brought it into the realm of the real? Potentially, I had just screwed up beyond all repair. Lost Josh and Dash in one horrifying, heartbreaking day.

I closed the computer with a click and tried to swallow against my suddenly dry throat.

"Maybe we should talk about something else," I said, my voice hollow.

Sabine laughed nervously. "Yes. Good idea."

We had come dangerously close to the abyss. It was time to turn back.

FOUR HOURS

That night I lay in bed, unable to sleep, staring at the ceiling. The images kept coming over and over. Cheyenne's bare legs. Josh's chest. Cheyenne climbing on top of him. His hand on her neck. On her shoulder. His eyes as he took her in. Her hands slowly unbuttoning her shirt. Her bra. Her thong. His unzipped pants . . .

I flipped over, face to pillow, and groaned. Tears squeezed their way out onto the pillowcase.

How could he do this to me? How?

I couldn't breathe. I lifted my head and my heart stopped. Red and blue lights flashed against the windowpane. A million flashback images from last year flooded my mind. I jumped from my bed and shoved the curtains aside.

There was an ambulance pulling past the girls' dormitory circle. I spotted it as it whizzed up the drive toward the end. Toward the second circle. Toward the boys' dorms. No siren. No noise. Just the silent scream of the lights.

I held my breath and clung to the curtains until it was out of sight. Then I opened the window and listened. Heard the distant pop of car doors closing. The sound of voices carrying through the clear night. And then, nothing.

I looked at the clock. Four hours until breakfast. Four hours to wait and wonder what the hell was going on now.

SWEET LITTLE SABINE

The next morning I was itching to get out in the world and find out what had happened, but I had to wait for Sabine. Considering the night I'd had, I was in no shape to traverse campus and deal with all the wagging tongues and curious eyes on my own. She dressed as quickly as she could, and we were just walking out of our room when we heard Cheyenne screech. There were pounding footsteps, and two seconds later she was in the hall in her pink bathrobe, clutching what looked like the tattered, stained, and slashed remains of the tartlet outfit Sabine had worn the day before.

"What is this?" she shouted at Sabine, storming over to us. She shook the garments in her fists.

"Oh, right. I tried to wash them since you were so kind as to let me borrow them, but the campus machine went crazy and just tore them all to shreds," Sabine said innocently.

My jaw dropped. She didn't. She couldn't. Sweet little Sabine?

"The washing machine did this," Cheyenne said facetiously. She unfurled the shirt and skirt. Each was cut into tiny little strips like fringe. And the stains on the shirt weren't just from juice and eggs. There were big black marks all over it, like the unfortunate person wearing it had been hit by a car.

Sabine shrugged. "It's an old machine."

"And I suppose it chewed my boots to pulp, too," Cheyenne said, glowering.

"No," Sabine said. "That was the janitor's dog. He busted into the laundry room and just grabbed them. There's no stopping a dog once he gets his teeth into real leather. I'm so sorry. I'll pay you back, of course."

I snorted a laugh. "I don't think that'll be necessary," I said, putting my arm over Sabine's shoulder. "I think the two of you are even now."

I turned Sabine around, and together we strolled for the door. "Thanks for that. I needed a laugh this morning," I said. "But I've gotta say, I didn't know you had it in you."

"Neither did I," Sabine replied. "But I suppose she just brings it out in me."

WASN'T ME

Every muscle in my body was tense as I walked to breakfast. Contrary to my plan, Sabine had bailed the moment we hit the front steps, needing to get some paperwork from her counselor, and I'd been left alone. Vulnerable. It was the first cool day of the year and I wasn't dressed for it. Hadn't even bothered to consider the weather. I shivered as a breeze rustled by, clinging to my bare arms. I looked around for distressed expressions, for whispering lips, for any indication of what had happened the night before. But all appeared normal. A sunny, happy Saturday at Easton Academy.

"Reed!"

Trey speed-walked over to me from the direction of Ketlar, his handsome face creased with concern. I stopped in my tracks. This could not be good.

"Are you all right? Have you heard from Josh?" he asked.

"What do you mean?"

He paused, confused. "Josh. They took him to the hospital last night. Didn't Gage call you?"

"No."

No, no, no.

"What happened?" I blurted.

"He had a seizure. I woke up out of nowhere and found him half falling out of his bed, shaking like crazy. I had to call 911," Trey said. "I'm sorry. Gage was supposed to—"

He stopped midsentence as a black sedan—one of Easton's official cars, used to retrieve visiting students and alumni from the airport—slid up the drive and paused between dorms. The door opened, and Josh stepped out very slowly. Jeans frayed, hair messed, but otherwise perfectly intact. The relief that flooded through me at the very sight of him was quickly obliterated the second he looked at me. In that second I recalled the anguish of last night. And I didn't care. I didn't care if he was fine or not. I just had to get out of there. I turned on my heel and stormed toward the dining hall, leaving Trey behind me.

"Reed! Wait!" Josh shouted.

I sped up.

"Reed! Please! I have to talk to you."

His hand fell on my shoulder. I whipped around, batting it away with my forearm in one motion.

"Ow! Dammit." He clung to his arm, slumped, like I'd just taken all the life out of him.

"We are done talking," I said through my teeth.

God, he looked pale. His eyes were all red and bloodshot. I wanted to hug him. Ask him what had happened. Had he been scared? I just wanted to kiss him and—

Smack him. No. Punch him. Right in the gut.

"Reed, I had a seizure last night," Josh told me, his tone pleading.

"And what? You want me to kiss you and make it all better?" I blurted, storming off again.

"No! That's not what I meant!" Josh said. "Please, Reed. Please just stop. I can't. I can't keep up with you right now."

There was something in his tone that stopped me. A pathetic quality that for some reason my heart couldn't ignore. When I looked at him again, he was sitting down on one of the stone benches. Slowly. Tenderly. As if every bone in his body hurt.

"What's the matter with you?" I asked belligerently.

"It's the seizure," he said. "All my muscles hurt. I think I just killed myself running to catch up with you."

He gave me a grimace/smile that brought angry tears to my eyes. Why was he doing this? Was he really expecting to get a pity vote that would somehow erase what he'd done?

"About last night," he said.

"I don't want to talk about it," I said.

"Well, I do," he snapped.

Snapped. At me. Like I was the one letting Cheyenne Martin crawl all over me.

"I was drugged, Reed. I didn't even know what the hell I was doing," he said, the words coming out in a rush. "I was in the art cemetery and all of a sudden she was there and then you were there and . . . I don't even remember half of it. I was completely out of it. You have to believe me. I would never do that to you. You know that. I don't even—"

"Stop," I said. My eyes were welling. Every pack of people that passed us by on the quad stared at us. "Stop lying."

"I'm not lying!" Josh shouted. "I'm telling you. Someone put something in my pillbox yesterday. I always set it up at the beginning of the week and sort the pills I need by day. Yesterday I dumped my pills into my hand and shoveled them into my mouth all at once. You've seen me do it a million times, right?"

Why was I still standing there? Why?

"Right?" he asked again.

I managed to nod.

"Well, right before they hit my mouth I noticed something. This small white pill with blue dots all over it. It wasn't one of my pills. But it was too late," he said, his eyes pleading. "I told myself I'd just imagined it, but now I know I didn't. It had to be one of those date rape drugs or something. It's the only explanation."

"Not the only one," I muttered.

"Why else would I have had a seizure last night?" Josh demanded. "Those have been under control for years. The only time I ever have one anymore is if I take something extra or drink too much or whatever. If my body chemistry gets thrown off. It makes perfect sense. Whatever I took . . . that threw me off enough to give me a seizure."

I stared down at him. At his hopeful green eyes. At his wan complexion.

"Somebody did this to me, Reed. To us," he said. "I would never willingly hurt you. You're everything to me, don't you get that? Everything."

My teeth clenched together so tightly, it sent my temple throbbing. "Then why did you text her?" I said quietly.

Josh blinked. "What?"

"Why did you text Cheyenne? You invited her there, Josh! You said you couldn't wait for her anymore. That you *needed* her!" I shouted. "If you were so taken advantage of, how the hell do you explain that?"

A few freshmen walking by stopped to stare. I didn't even care. Let them see what happened when you let yourself care about someone. Let me be a cautionary tale. Something good should come out of my crap-ass life.

"Reed, I have no idea what you're talking about," Josh said.

"Stop lying!" I practically screamed. "I saw it on her phone! She showed it to me. It came from your cell. You invited her there!"

"I didn't. I didn't," Josh rambled, shaking his head. Squinting his eyes. As if trying to remember. "We were at a committee meeting in Mitchell Hall for the Driscoll dinner thing. After it was over I went to the cemetery. She followed me in there. She followed me—"

"Please stop," I said, tears spilling over onto my cheeks. "I can't stand here and listen to this anymore."

I turned around, hugging myself, and walked away. He stood up, but winced and didn't move.

"Reed, please don't do this. It wasn't me. I didn't know what I was doing," he pleaded. "I love you! Reed! You know that I love you!"

My heart tore down the middle. Today his words felt like a cruel joke. Like torture. He kept calling to me, but I didn't look back. I would never look back.

THE BEST

I sat up straight in bed when the front door of Billings slammed closed. The first thing I noticed was that Sabine was not in her bed. The second was the time on the clock: 1:04 a.m. Then I heard Mr. White's icy voice down in the lobby. Sound really carried in an old, creaky house like this one. Especially when no one was attempting to be quiet.

"To bed," he said. "Now."

"Crap," I said under my breath, flinging my sheets aside.

Several footfalls on the stairs told me Sabine was not alone. When the door opened, Constance and Lorna were with her. Their heads were all bowed.

"What the hell—"

I didn't get the chance to finish my sentence.

"What the hell happened?" Cheyenne howled, tearing in wearing nothing but a short pink nightgown. She was followed by London,

Vienna, Portia, Rose, Tiffany, Missy, and Astrid. I hadn't spoken to her all day, and part of me wanted to grab her and shove her right back out of my room.

"No one invited you in here," I spat. No one even looked at me.

"We got caught," Constance told us as she shrugged out of her jacket.

"What?" Cheyenne whisper-screeched.

"Oh, this is just brill," Portia blurted, touching her diamond *B*. "I knew this was going to happen!"

"Caught doing what?" I demanded, heart pounding.

"They were supposed to be stealing a test," Portia explained.

"Are you expelled?" Cheyenne demanded of the three of them. There was obvious hope behind her eyes.

"No," Sabine said bitterly, knowing, as she did, that Cheyenne wanted her gone. "They caught us outside. Lorna said we were out for a midnight stroll, and they couldn't prove otherwise. We're only on probation."

"Quick thinking, Lorna," Tiffany said, rousing a rare but weak smile from Lorna.

"Probation?" Rose asked. "Meaning what, exactly?"

"Mr. White said if any of the three of us steps one more foot out of line, we're gone," Constance explained. She looked as if her life was flashing before her eyes.

"Unbelievable," Cheyenne said, throwing up her hands. "Do you know that in the eighty-plus years that Billings House has been functioning not a single person has gotten caught on this task? It's a veritable cake walk!"

Shut up, you backstabbing bitch. Shut up, shut up, shut up!

"I would never have gotten caught," Missy sniffed.

I stared at her. Every inch of my skin tingled. She stood in the middle of my room in a pair of silk pajama pants and a tank top. Astrid, too, was in boxer shorts. Kiki wasn't even there, probably still sleeping. But Constance, Sabine, and Lorna were dressed in head-to-toe black. "Why didn't you get caught?" I asked.

"Excuse me?" Missy snapped.

"Why weren't you out there with them?" I asked, then looked at Cheyenne. It took some effort to do that without retching, but I forced myself. "If every Billings Girl has passed this task since the beginning of time, why weren't Missy and Astrid and Kiki out trying to pass it?"

Cheyenne scoffed. "I couldn't exactly send six girls out at once to tromp around campus, could I?" she said, tugging on her hair. "The others were going to go out tomorrow night. Not that they can *now*," she added, casting a disgusted look at the three in black. "Nice to ruin it for everyone."

Sabine, Lorna, and Constance looked at their feet, like kinder-gartners who'd just gotten caught raiding the cookie jar. This was so degrading. So humiliating. And they so did not deserve it.

You have the high road, I thought, hearing Dash's voice in my head.

"All right. That's it," I said. "Cheyenne. Outside."

There was no getting around it. We lived in the same house. She was systematically torturing my friends. I was going to have to deal with her. But if I was going to have to deal with her, it would be on my terms.

"What?" she snapped.

"You, me, let's go."

"No way. Not if you're going to go all *Million Dollar Baby* on me again," she said, paling.

"I won't touch you. I swear," I said, standing at the doorway. "We're just going to have a little chat."

She looked at her friends as if to make sure they'd have her back if I threw down, then swooped by me out the door. I cringed at her close proximity as images of her and Josh assaulted me again. Taking a deep breath, I pushed them aside and closed the door. I tucked my clenched fists under my arms and turned to face off with Cheyenne. She took an instinctive step back in the hallway, toward her room. It was all I could do to keep from laughing at her tremulousness.

"This ends now," I said.

She laughed. Loudly. Probably relieved that I wasn't right-hooking her jaw. "You're out of your mind."

"No, I think I'm actually in my right mind for the first time all year," I told her. "You are going to back off those girls starting right now, or I'm going to the headmaster to tell him that you're orchestrating all of this. That this is all part of the sorority thing you've created around here that he hates so much."

She laughed again, until she saw the fire in my eyes. "You wouldn't."

"Wouldn't I?" I asked. "After everything you've done to me, do you really think I would hesitate a second to carry through on that threat?"

Cheyenne studied me. I could practically hear the gears in her head creaking.

"I'd tell everyone it was you," she said, lifting her chin. "Everyone in Billings would know that you went against your own."

"Somehow, after last night, I don't think they would blame me."

"Oh, they would. These girls are remarkably self-centered, if you haven't noticed. They'll start wondering about you. If you can back-stab me, then who's next?" Cheyenne theorized. "Do those losers really matter more to you than Billings does?"

"No," I told her firmly. "But they do matter more to me than you." Her jaw dropped slightly and her cheeks turned crimson. How she could be surprised at this, I had no idea, but I stepped even closer to her, sensing I had her just where I wanted her. "I'll deal with the rest of the house if and when the time comes. But I'm sure the headmaster would much rather pull one lonely troublemaker out of Billings than have to close down the whole dorm and explain that to the prestigious Billings alumnae, don't you think?"

Her eyes were wide. I had never seen Cheyenne speechless before.

"I know how much you love this place," I said. "I know how much it would kill you to have to go live in Pemberly with the commoners."

"You can't."

"Oh, I can." I felt strong as I stared her down. Certain. I had the high road. I was in charge. "Don't test me, Cheyenne. I learned from the best."

With that, I turned around and went back into my room, slamming the door in her face. Finally, I had gotten the last word.

ADEQUATE

Between my bio lab and chem class I received a text from Rose telling me to come straight back to Billings after soccer practice for a meeting. I spent the entire time on the field missing passes, shooting wide, and falling all over myself, my mind on other things. On Josh. On Cheyenne. On their gut-crushing betrayal. And on this meeting. What could it possibly be about? I couldn't even begin to hazard a guess, but considering my current frame of mind, I knew it couldn't be good.

"How're you holding up?" Astrid asked me as we tromped down the hill back toward the school buildings.

Her question made my fists clench. She was, after all, friends with the enemy. Why was she asking? So she could report back to Cheyenne?

"I'm fine," I said flatly.

"Reed, I'm not on her side," Astrid said, stopping in her tracks.

It took me a few more steps to pause. I held my breath as I looked at her, but I had no idea what to say.

"I think that she's a complete cow for what she did," Astrid told me, tucking her soccer ball under her arm. "We never were proper friends, just people who knew each other through our families, and at this point I feel quite sure we never will be."

My heart felt squishy and warm and distrustful at the same time. "I don't know what to say."

"I don't blame you for not trusting me, but one day you will," Astrid said, completely unfazed. "I have a way of growing on people."

She winked and I laughed. "Okay. Fair enough."

Her cell phone beeped and she pulled it from her duffel bag and groaned. "Bollocks."

"What is it?" I asked.

"Text from the Nazi herself. Says all the newbies are to go directly to the library and wait for further instruction. Bloody hell. I was looking forward to a shower."

All the little hairs on my neck stood on end. What the hell was going on? It was all I could do to keep from running to Billings to find out, but I didn't want Astrid to think I was not in the know. I walked her to the split in the path, then speed-walked my way into the house.

There was a lot of chatter coming from the parlor. Glasses clinked, girls giggled, general sounds of merriment. I walked over to the doorway and found every last one of my housemates, minus the six new girls, gathered around a tray of lemonade, chattering away. I'd just walked into a WASP-athon.

"Reed! There you are!" Vienna called out. She quickly poured me a crystal tumbler full of lemonade and got up to present it to me. Tiffany snapped our picture. "Now we can get started!"

I dropped my soccer bag on the floor. "Started with what, exactly?"

"Planning the initiation ceremony," Rose said.

"I get to be in charge of invitations!" London trilled happily, fanning herself with a stationery catalog.

"I thought we weren't having initiation," I said. "Didn't the headmaster basically forbid it?" Like that mattered anymore, but still. Someone had to say it.

"There are certain traditions we must uphold," Cheyenne said, walking around the couch and settee to stand in front of me. If she had been intimidated by me the night before, she wasn't showing it now. It was amazing how my blood boiled at the very sight of her. Her and her smug, prissy face. All day, every time I laid eyes on her, all I could think about was her and Josh. Were they together now? A couple? He'd been sitting exclusively at the Ketlar table, avoiding us both like we were contagious, but who knew if they were meeting in secret? Who knew what they had done together? She'd killed the best thing in my life. Stolen my boyfriend. And now here she was lecturing me about something as ridiculous as tradition.

"That's great, Cheyenne, except when the keeping-up-tradition could get us all expelled," I said finally.

A few of the girls exchanged looks, as if this hadn't occurred to them before. I looked down my nose at Cheyenne, straightening to full height. All the better to remind her of how scary I could be.

"Let's look at it this way, Reed," Cheyenne said, placing her palms together. She looked at me with pity, like she was talking to an addled old woman. "How would you feel if you'd had to miss out on the experience of your Billings initiation just because some new headmaster randomly decided to crack down?"

She had me there. As odd and frightening and unexpected as my initiation had been at first, it had also been fairly cool. It had been the first time at Easton that I had actually felt as if I belonged somewhere. As if I was wanted. But then there was that small question of the vote. Of the fact that some of the girls were not technically wanted at all.

"Let me ask you this," I said. "Who, exactly, are we initiating?"

"All of them!" Rose announced happily.

"Really?" I was stunned.

"We all talked it over before you got here and we decided you were right," Cheyenne said, just about containing the sour look in her eyes. "We can't fight the headmaster on this. And it's not like they're lepers or something. They're all . . . adequate."

"And we can work on the ones who aren't," London added.

Translation? I'd won. Cheyenne had seen it in my eyes the night before that I meant business. I had actually intimidated someone into submission. My heart welled with pride. It was all I could do to keep from happy-dancing around her like she were a sombrero. Maybe she had taken Josh, but I had taken her pride. It was a small victory.

"And we can't spend the entire year working against these girls. We do have other things to focus on. Applications, senior events . . ."

She glanced at me in an almost teasing way, and I felt my face turn red. Josh. She was thinking about Josh. Mocking me about him.

Take the high road, Reed. Don't tear her hair out just yet. She's conceding the war to you right now. She's just trying to save face.

"Fine. I'm glad you finally came around," I told her. "But we cannot let the headmaster find out about this."

"Well, obvi," Portia said, rolling her big brown eyes.

I would *love* to see Portia in a job interview. Seriously. Not that she would ever have to go through one.

"Now, let's get to work," Cheyenne said. "We have a big event to plan and not much time."

As much as I still wanted to throttle Cheyenne, I couldn't help smiling as I joined the rest of the Billings Girls. I had won. Billings would be a better place because of me. I had beaten Cheyenne.

How I wished Noelle could see me now.

FAMILIAR

Tiffany struggled to catch up with me as we walked to class after lunch. I had been hyperaware of Josh staring at me from across the cafeteria, and I needed to get away as fast as I could. No way I wanted another dramatic encounter. I just wanted it to be done. Done and over and forgotten.

"Reed! Reed, wait up!"

It was him. My steps hurried forward.

"Reed, you need to take this up as an Olympic sport," Tiffany told me, breathless at my side.

"Reed! Please don't do this!"

"I'm sorry, Tiffany. I gotta go."

I started running. I knew I looked insane, with my hair whipping around and my heavy bag banging against my side, but I didn't care. I was halfway up the steps to the class building when he caught up to me. Grabbed my sleeve. A couple of sophomores on their way inside looked at me, alarmed, and I averted my gaze.

"What do you want, Josh?"

I made the mistake of looking at him. God, he was gorgeous. Even more so when I couldn't have him. Couldn't touch him. Couldn't kiss him. He was supposed to be dead to me. How could he be so beautiful?

"We have to talk about this," he said, heaving for air. His eyes were desperate. Pleading. "This can't just be over. It can't."

My heart was choking me. I had to get out of there. "But it is. It is over. You have to leave me alone."

I had never seen anyone look so crushed. Maybe it was all true. Maybe he had been drugged. Maybe it wasn't his fault. . . .

No. No. I was not going there. I was not going to be the idiot. He'd broken my heart. No one got a second chance to do that. Not again.

"I have to go."

"Reed—"

Tiffany caught up with us then, thank God. She put her arm through mine and stared him down. "We're leaving."

That was all I needed. I turned and shoved through the doors. I had only taken two shaky steps inside when a voice stopped me.

"Breaking hearts again, Brennan?"

It was Ivy Slade. Standing behind us near the door, slim arms crossed over her slim chest. Amused. Challenging.

"Who the hell do you think you are? You don't even know me!" I blurted, getting right in her face.

I was already so pent up from the encounter with Josh, I was practically grateful to her for giving me a reason to explode. But she didn't even flinch.

"Oh, I know you. I know you better than you can possibly imagine."

It took a good five seconds for any of this to process. By the time it did, Tiffany was trying to tug me away. "Don't listen to her, Reed. It's pointless."

But I couldn't walk away now. "What do you mean?" I asked her. "Who told you about me? Taylor? Are you still in touch with Taylor Bell?"

Her thin lips twisted into a smirk.

"You are, aren't you? Where is she? What the hell happened to her?" I asked, feeling wild and out of control in the face of her complete calm. "What did she tell you about me?"

"Classic Reed," she said. "Always so full of questions."

I saw red. I couldn't believe this girl was standing there talking down to me like this. Talking as if she knew anything about me.

"Who the hell *are* you?" I demanded.

She simply smiled and stepped around us, walking slowly and unaffectedly down the hall. Turning her back on me like I was so unworthy of her time.

"Bitch," Tiffany said under her breath.

I was shaking from head to toe. "What just happened?" I asked her. "What is that girl's deal?"

"Reed, breathe," Tiffany told me.

I did. I sucked in air. Didn't realize until that moment that I hadn't done that for a while.

"Good. Now listen to me," Tiffany said, her brown eyes serious. "Do not spend one extra second thinking about Ivy Slade. She's just messing with you."

"But why?" I asked.

"Because it's what she does," Tiffany said, looking down the hall after the girl. "It's pretty much what she lives for."

Ivy paused at the door of a classroom, flipped her long black hair back, and smiled knowingly. A chill enveloped my insides, and fear gripped my heart. I practically fell onto the bench near the wall.

"Reed? Are you okay?" Tiffany asked.

"I'm fine. I'm fine. It's just been an emotional couple of minutes," I told her.

"Should I get the nurse? Do you need water?" she asked.

I must have looked really bad to merit that reaction. I tipped forward and put my head between my knees. I was fine. Or I would be. I just had to let this feeling pass. This eerily familiar feeling.

This feeling I hadn't felt since the last time I'd looked into Ariana Osgood's eyes.

JUST A DORM

"What's the matter?" I asked Sabine as she caught up to me on the steps of the library later that day. The sun was just dipping below the horizon, and the tiny lights that lined the stone pathways flickered on, casting a warm, welcoming glow. It was a beautiful late-summer evening. I, however, couldn't wait to get inside. All day, whenever I was out in the open. I felt like a gazelle in the middle of lion country, always afraid that Josh was about to come around the corner or that Ivy would find me again and systematically pick apart my brain. Sabine, however, looked even more stressed than I felt. "Is it Cheyenne? What did she do now?"

"No. I just found out I have to pick a sport." She pulled a face, like the idea of physical exertion was disgusting to her.

"You don't play anything?" I asked, opening the door for her.

"Not really," she said. "Tennis, a bit, but that's in the spring. I have to do something now."

"Why don't you join the soccer team?" I suggested.

She guffawed. "Oh, because I know nothing about soccer and have a fear of large girls with a lust for blood?"

I laughed. "Nice picture. But it doesn't matter. Astrid's on the team and she's not much of an athlete. There are always a few who just ride the bench. You could be one of those people."

"Maybe . . ." Her face brightened slightly. "Okay. I will think about it. Thanks, Reed."

I smiled as we found ourselves a table, the whole Josh thing momentarily reduced to a minor ache. I was so glad Sabine had decided to come to Easton of all the schools in New England.

"Omigod, you guys!"

Constance came tearing around the stacks, all wild-haired and bright-eyed, like something cute and hyper out of a Disney cartoon.

"Look what I got!" she exclaimed.

She sat down next to me and slid a small ivory card out of her notebook. Sabine sat back when she saw it, uninterested, but I picked it up. It was of thick stock and had very few words printed on it in a swirling script.

Constance Talbot
The Sisters of Billings House
Request the Honor of Your Presence
in the Billings Parlor
Ten o'clock
Tonight
Wear only white

"Did your invitation look like that?" Constance asked breathlessly.

"Actually my invitation looked like a half-empty dorm room, remember?" I said.

"Oh, yeah. Right. But this is it, right? Initiation?" she whispered, looking around. "Are we going to get our diamond *B*s there?"

I smiled, so glad that all the uncertainty and anguish were about to end for her. "I guess you'll have to show up and find out," I said with a conspiratorial smile.

Constance giggled uncontrollably and slipped the invite away. Across the table, Sabine sighed.

"What's the matter?" I asked, a sudden suspicion occurring to me. "You did get one, didn't you?"

"Yes. But I just don't understand," she said petulantly. "I didn't ask to be in some sorority. It's just a dorm. A place to live. A place they put me. And now I have to go through all these tests and rituals, just to be accepted in the house I was sent to. It doesn't seem fair."

Constance and I exchanged a look. "You don't want to be in Billings?" Constance demanded, dumbfounded.

Sabine lifted a shoulder, and I felt this weird twinge. This irritation at being rejected. How could anyone not want to be in Billings?

But then, Sabine was an outsider. She hadn't had the superiority of Billings House drilled into her from day one like I had. She had never met Noelle, Ariana, Kiran, and Taylor. Never seen how seductive and cool the Billings Girls could truly be. She had just been shown through the door at the feet of substandards like Cheyenne and Portia and had been either tortured or publicly humiliated every day since. Why *should* she look up to them—to us? To her we were just a bunch of random girls forcing her to do random crap for our approval.

"Sabine, if you don't want to do it, you don't have to," I told her, feeling almost sacrilegious, but forging ahead. "I'm sure you can get a transfer. There are other rooms on campus."

Even though I'd hate, hate, *hate* to see Cheyenne win.

"Yes, but then . . ." She looked away and toyed with her pen, as if embarrassed by what she was about to say.

"But then what?" Constance prompted.

"But then I would not be rooming with you," she said, looking at me.

Now I felt a *real* pang.

"Aw!" Constance trilled, giving us both a little pouty look. "I was the same way last year when she left me. She's, like, the *best* roommate."

I laughed and shook my head. They were ridiculous, but I was pleased nonetheless. "Don't worry, Sabine. It'll get better. After tonight, it'll get *a lot* better. I promise."

Sabine nodded, seeming comforted. I only hoped that my promise didn't turn out to be a false one.

NEW RITUAL

I stood between Vienna and Rose that night, dressed in my basic black skirt and a black ballet-neck T-shirt, my hair pulled back from my face. Rose wore a simple black dress, but Vienna was, as ever, busting out the top of a strapless black frock that could have been a pillowcase in a former life. Around us, the rest of the Billings Girls were gathered into a semicircle, our black taper candles flickering in front of us. All except Cheyenne, who had taken Noelle's position before us. Her face seemed to be set in a permanent smirk.

We heard footsteps creaking at the top of the stairs. My pulse started to race.

"Here we go," Rose said under her breath.

"Shhh!" Cheyenne admonished.

Rose rolled her eyes.

Finally, London appeared on the steps, wearing a slightly more modest dress than her Twin City counterpart. Ever-so-slowly, she led the six new Billings Girls down the stairs and into the foyer. They were blindfolded and holding hands in a line. All in white, they looked like a string of freshly cut paper dolls. When London stopped, they all bumped into one another one by one, and even I had a hard time keeping myself from laughing. London slipped over to stand next to Vienna. Constance's head twitched around nervously, and I was so elated for her. In a few minutes all her uncertainty would be over. I couldn't wait.

"Ladies. Remove your blindfolds," Cheyenne ordered, lowering her voice to what was supposed to be an imperious tone. She sounded more shrill than intimidating.

The girls tore off their white blindfolds. They looked around, confused and blinking. Constance's eyes fell on the jewelry boxes that sat on the mantel and I saw her bite down on her lip to keep from smiling.

"Welcome, everyone, to this, the eighty-fifth initiation ceremony of Billings House," Cheyenne said. "You will each step forward when I call your name."

My candle warmed my face as someone down the line cursed under her breath, burned by hot wax. It was amazing, seeing the ritual from this side. It had seemed so eerie and important last year. The girls all so ethereal and untouchable. Now I knew they were just a bunch of girls who were stressing about their homework, picking their wedgies, and looking forward to the champagne stashed in the next room.

"Step forward, Astrid Chou," Cheyenne said.

Astrid stepped up. Cheyenne handed her an unlit candle, which Astrid tipped toward Cheyenne's to accept the flame.

"Ladies of Billings House, do we receive Astrid Chou into our circle?" Cheyenne asked.

"Welcome, Astrid! To our circle!" we chorused.

We had gone over it just before the ceremony, but somehow, it still sounded different to me. Different from my initiation. But then, a lot of this was different. I had been all alone. I hadn't been blindfolded and dressed in white. I had been a last-minute substitution. And to be honest, the details of that intense day were still very murky.

Astrid smiled as Portia retrieved a jewelry box from the pile and opened it to reveal the diamond *B* inside. Astrid grinned and took the box in her free hand. Cheyenne touched her shoulder, steering her toward the end of the semicircle. She was now on our side of the room. One of us.

"Step forward, Melissa Thurber," Cheyenne said.

Missy's nose was so high in the air, she could probably smell tomorrow morning's breakfast. We went through the ritual again.

"Ladies of Billings House, do we receive Melissa Thurber into our circle?"

"Welcome, Melissa! To our circle."

I may not have said it so loudly that time.

Missy received her necklace and stood next to Astrid. We initiated Kiki, who was wearing her Easton tennis uniform—probably the only piece of white clothing she owned—and then it was Sabine's turn.

"Step forward, Sabine DuLac," Cheyenne said.

The flame of her candle flickered. Between the dancing shadows I could have sworn I saw a mischievous gleam in her eye. My heart skipped a beat, but I told myself I was seeing things. I had to be seeing things.

"Ladies of Billings House, do we receive Sabine DuLac into our circle?" Cheyenne asked, looking over at us.

"Welcome, Sabine! To our circle!"

All the oxygen was sucked out of the room. Rose, Tiffany, London, and I were the only ones who had spoken. The lobby was so deathly silent, I could hear the candle flames hissing. Sabine's skin had turned waxy in the dim light.

"London!" Vienna said through her teeth.

"Sorry! I forgot," London whispered back.

I opened my mouth to speak, but Portia's sudden movement startled me. She grabbed a box from the mantel, opened it, and handed it to Sabine. Sabine's hand trembled as she reached for it. There was nothing inside.

"Step forward, Constance Talbot!" Cheyenne said, hurrying things along.

"Wait," I heard myself say.

This was wrong. This was all wrong.Constance looked petrified as she stood next to Sabine. Petrified but still somehow hopeful. I thought Cheyenne had caved. I thought my threat had worked. But this—

"Ladies of Billings House, do we receive Constance Talbot into our circle?" Cheyenne asked.

Dead. Silence.

"Welcome, Constance! To our circle!" I said loudly.

Constance received her empty box.

"Step forward, Lorna Gross."

Lorna didn't move. Her head was tipped forward. She was already sobbing. That was it. Never in my life had I seen anything quite this cruel. And I couldn't help feeling that this was my fault. That I had been so naïve as to believe that my tactics had worked on Cheyenne. What had I been thinking? She was the only person I had ever seen get one over on Noelle Lange. It had only happened once, but it had happened. How could I have thought myself better than that?

"Stop this!" I shouted.

I stepped out of line and faced Cheyenne, shaking with barely restrained rage.

"Reed. Get back in line," Cheyenne ordered.

"You uncontrollable bitch," I said, my jaw clenched. "You can't do this to them."

"Reed! You're disrupting an ages-old ritual!" Cheyenne lifted her hand to her chest, faking shock.

"Screw your ritual!" I shouted. I blew out my candle and threw it at her feet, where it broke in two. "This is *not* how your precious founding sisters would want this place to be!"

"Oh, please. Like you know anything about Billings and its history," Cheyenne spat. "My grandmother was in Billings. My mother. All her friends. And if they knew how you and our new headmaster were trying to corrupt it, they'd be appalled."

"I think they'd be appalled by you," I retorted.

"That's it. I'm done playing nice with you," Cheyenne said,

stepping up to me. "You don't belong here, Reed. No more than any of these losers do."

"What?" I snapped.

"You know it. We all know it. No one here voted you in. You were Ariana's pet project. She went over all our heads to get Leanne expelled and bring you in, but guess what? Ariana—psycho that she turned out to be—is gone now. And nobody wants you here."

I stared at her, unable to find the words to cut through my fury. "You're wrong."

"Am I?"

She was. She had to be. And yet, no one was coming to my defense. I stared into Cheyenne's eyes defiantly, just willing someone, anyone, to stick up for me. No one did. Well, screw them. Sure, maybe they had all gone through all the hazing and ridiculous chores and tests, but I had nearly died to be here. Not another soul in that room could claim that. I was more of a Billings Girl than any of them.

"Uh, Reed?" Rose said. "Cheyenne?"

"What?" we both blurted.

We turned to look at her, and our jaws dropped in unison. Suddenly I knew why not even my closest allies had spoken up. Standing at the open door were Headmaster Cromwell, his goon Mr. White, and our housemother Mrs. Lattimer, clutching at the high neck of her blouse. The headmaster looked around, taking in the candles, the black and white clothing, the discarded blindfolds, and set his face into a grim mask.

"Well," he said finally. "This is very disappointing."

RINGLEADER

Headmaster Cromwell and I stared at each other across his wide desk. A fire crackled in the huge stone fireplace behind me, heating my back to the point of blistering. It was twenty past midnight. He and Mr. White had already grilled most of my Billings sisters. They had each passed me by in the outer waiting room, heads down, no eye contact. Not one of them had looked at me or Cheyenne, who was still on the other side of that thick wooden door. Waiting.

If he was going to expel me, I wished he would just get it over with. The skin on my neck was going to be permanently disfigured at this point.

The headmaster shifted in his seat, leaning back and placing one finger on his cheek as he studied me. If he was waiting for me to crack and start blubbering, he had no idea who he was dealing with. My stomach was folding over and over and over on itself like an intricate work of origami, and I had to pee. My palms were sweating. My head pounded. My eyes were dry. But none of that mattered. I'd already read all the titles on the 234 tomes behind his desk, and I could do it again. He had them in alphabetical order by author, OCD man that he was. Perfectly in order. Just like the rest of his office. All right angles, gleaming glass, and freshly shone wood.

Behind me, Mr. White cleared his throat. The headmaster looked up. He adjusted back to his original position. Hands laced together on his desk. Expression stern.

"What was going on in Billings House tonight, Miss Brennan?" he asked in that imperious voice of his.

I smirked. "You've already talked to fourteen of my friends. I think you know."

His eyebrows arched. Oops. Too pert? But we both knew this was a joke. Someone had obviously cracked before I even walked through his door. Constance, definitely, could never have handled this. So why was he even continuing with this charade?

"I'd like to hear it from you," he said.

"I have nothing to say," I told him.

He blew out a sigh. "Look, Miss Brennan, I'm not here to make trouble for you. I know your history. I've read your file. I hardly believe that a scholarship student from central Pennsylvania is the ringleader of this little sorority of yours. All I want to know is who that ringleader might be. Tell me that, and then you can go."

I almost choked on a laugh. Was he really good-copping me? And even more ridiculous, was he really telling me that all I had to do was give up the one girl I wanted to see booted from this institution and I was off the hook? It was almost too perfect.

"I know who it is, Miss Brennan. You know who it is," he told me. "But I need someone to go on record with the information if I'm going to do anything about it."

So it was up to me. No one else had given her up. That was what he was telling me. Shocking. Finally it had come down to me and Cheyenne. I could end this, right here, right now. Get rid of the girl who had stolen the love of my life. Make it so that she and Josh would never see each other again. Well, maybe not never, but at least not every day. Get them out of trysting distance of each other. Oh, how I'd love to take away any possibility Cheyenne had of being with him again.

But the more I thought about it, a cold blanket descended over my shoulders. As much as I hated her, as awful as she'd been, as easily as she'd tricked me, now that I was faced with the choice, I knew that I couldn't be the one to give up Cheyenne. Doing that would be proving her right about me. It would be proving to her that I wasn't a true Billings Girl. That I didn't understand what it meant. Maybe I didn't agree with all Cheyenne's opinions on what being in Billings signi-fied, but I did know one thing. Billings Girls protected one another. Even when they didn't want to. I'd learned that from Noelle. Among so many other things. The only reason to turn Cheyenne in now would be to protect myself, and I had a feeling that I wasn't going anywhere. As long as we stuck together, the headmaster could do nothing. There was no way he could expel sixteen of us without a negative backlash from the alumni and the press unlike any other.

"So, Miss Brennan. What's it going to be?" the headmaster asked me, looking quite sure of himself. "Are you going to tell me whose idea it was to have this initiation?"

I sat up straight, looked him dead in the eye, and smiled. His expression of certainty faltered. I wished Cheyenne were here to witness this.

"Headmaster Cromwell," I said. "I have no idea what you're talking about."

DONE

When I got back to Billings, everyone was gathered in the parlor. Everyone except Cheyenne, who had been called into the headmaster's office after me. Rose and Portia stood up when I walked in. Portia's eyes darted behind me.

"Where's Cheyenne?" she asked.

"Still there."

I was suddenly exhausted. I walked over to the bay window and sat down, staring out at the darkened quad. There were too many thoughts. Impossible to focus. What had I done? Had I really passed by my chance to rid my life of Cheyenne? Was I really going to have to live with all that hatred for the rest of the year?

I felt a hand touch my shoulder and looked up. It was Rose.

"I just wanted to see if you're okay," she said. "After everything Cheyenne said before . . ."

My heart felt hollow. "Thanks. I'm fine."

Behind her the rest of the girls started to murmur amongst themselves. Constance, Sabine, Astrid, Kiki, and Lorna were all gathered in a corner, talking urgently. Missy sat alone, staring into the darkened fireplace.

"It's not true, you know. What she said," Rose told me, sitting across from me in the window bench. "Well, part of it is. You weren't voted in the normal way. But she was wrong when she said no one wants you there. We all love you."

I had to laugh. I leaned my head on the cool windowpane and looked out. "Yeah, right."

"I'm serious," Rose told me. "After everything you went through last year, just the fact that you came back spring semester . . . Well, everyone was impressed. I mean, none of us could have been that brave. You know everyone likes you. We had so much fun last spring. The spa trips, that insane shopping weekend in Boston, Vienna's sweet-seventeen party."

I smiled, recalling how Vienna had gotten so wasted, she'd decided to try to reinvent her balance beam routine from her brief childhood flirtation with gymnastics. Problem being she had tried to create it on the railing of her father's yacht while out at sea. Gage had caught her about two seconds before going over, then made everyone call him "My Savior" all night long. Because, in his opinion, his great achievement was saving the party for all of us. Not saving Vienna's life.

"It's just Cheyenne," Rose told me. "For whatever reason, she's had issues with you from day one."

"I think we both know the reason. She's never thought a scholarship student with a Gap wardrobe and a twenty-dollar haircut belonged in Billings," I said, remembering that day during my hazing that Cheyenne had referred to my blue-collar background and crushed her blush beads into her rug for me to clean up. Somehow, between then and now, I had allowed myself to forget about that. Had even enjoyed her company some last year. Temporary insanity.

"Twenty dollars? Really?" Rose said, looking momentarily horrified. Then she recalled herself and waved her hand. "I mean, you totally can't tell."

"Thanks, Rose," I said with a laugh.

"No problem!" Rose trilled. "So we're good?"

I didn't have the chance to respond. The front door of Billings opened. Cheyenne walked into the parlor, her steps stiff, her eyes red. She looked as if she'd just been told she had two weeks to live.

"What happened?" Rose asked, standing.

"I'm out," Cheyenne said. She stared straight ahead, not meeting anyone's eye. "I'm expelled."

The air was forcibly sucked from my lungs. I couldn't move. I had no idea what to think.

"But you didn't do anything!" Portia said. "At least, nothing we haven't always done. Did you tell him—"

"They don't care," Cheyenne said, lifting her eyes for the first time. "They didn't even want to hear it. I have tonight to pack my things, and tomorrow I'm gone."

She turned around and staggered out. Portia leapt over Tiffany's legs and scurried to follow. No one else moved. I looked over at Sabine, trembling. Sabine stared back. It was over. Cheyenne had gotten herself expelled. And we hadn't done a thing.

PUNISHMENT FITTING
THE CRIME

Two seconds later no one had recovered enough to move, and once again the front door of Billings opened. Our eyes darted everywhere, like our fortress was being invaded and no one knew where the weapons were. Headmaster Cromwell walked right into the parlor with Mrs. Naylor, of all people, on his heels. It was the middle of the night and she was fully dressed in a gray suit and eggplant shirt, her watery eyes heavily lined as always.

"Everyone please sit," the headmaster ordered.

We did. All fourteen of us. I wondered if he would notice Portia's absence, but didn't much care. What now? My heart wasn't going to be able to take many more moments like this. There was no air in the room. My pulse was shallow and rapid. To my left, Sabine was so tense, a loud noise would have sent her straight through the ceiling. To my right, Constance looked green. Tiffany's hands were folded on her lap. Her camera, for once, was nowhere in sight.

The headmaster cleared his throat. "Ladies, I think you already know how gravely disappointed I am, so I'm not going to rehash that now," Cromwell began. "You should all know that Cheyenne Martin has been expelled and I've fired Mrs. Lattimer."

Gasps all around. Even I couldn't believe that one.

"I realize she's been with the school for a number of years, but clearly she was unable to control you, and so she had to go."

"Omigod," Vienna said under her breath.

I knew what she was thinking. Lattimer may have been haughty and prim, but she had also been in our pocket. She had looked the other way on several occasions, not just this year, but last year as well. It had always been implied that Noelle was slipping her money or shoes or whatever it was she wanted in order to buy her cooperation. If she was gone . . .

"Mrs. Naylor has kindly volunteered to take Mrs. Lattimer's place," the headmaster continued.

Mrs. Naylor lifted her head. Her waddle swung back and forth beneath her chin as she looked down at us. Constance grabbed my hand, probably to keep from flinching.

"Mrs. Naylor will be writing up daily reports about the goings-on inside Billings," the headmaster continued. "Reports which I will read every night. When one of you sneezes, I will know about it. If there is so much as an unkind word spoken between you, I will know about it. So I suggest you start thinking seriously about how you're going to conduct yourselves from this moment forward. Mrs. Naylor, you have the floor."

The headmaster stepped aside, and Mrs. Naylor strode back and forth along the front window, eyeing us like new recruits into her personal army of pain. Her orthopedic shoes had been shined to a gleam, and they squished and squeaked as she walked.

"Many of you know me," she began. "Some of you do not. For those of you who do not, rest assured you will get to know me. Well. You and I will be spending *a lot* of time together. This school is a respected institution of learning. Your dorm rooms are for studying and for sleeping. They are not for socializing. They are not for partying. As far as I am concerned, you and your lot have done enough to sully the good name of Easton Academy over the past few years. That all ends with me."

I glanced at London and Vienna, who both looked as if they'd just had their American Express Black cards taken away. The desperation in the air was palpable.

As punishments went, I had to admit, this one was creative. Cromwell hadn't expelled us, but to most of my housemates, this was even worse. If they had been expelled, they could have moved on to one of the many other posh boarding schools and continued to party like the celebutantes they were. But with Mrs. Naylor breathing down our necks, the party was over. Life in Billings House would never be the same.

PEACE

The door to Cheyenne's room was open. I don't know what drew me there, but while everyone else followed Mrs. Naylor's orders to go directly to bed, I went to Cheyenne's doorway. I was breathless, knowing what this must be doing to her. She loved this place. Not just Billings House, but Easton. This was her senior year. And just like that, it was all over.

I found Cheyenne sitting on the edge of her neat-as-a-pin bed, knees together, feet apart, posture slumped. Just staring. Her eyes flicked to me.

"Come to gloat?" she asked.

"No," I said automatically.

"Why not? Isn't this what you wanted?" she asked, lifting her palms as she stood. "Isn't this what you've been working for all year?"

I blinked. "Working for? You were the one who was trying to get people thrown out. I was just defending them."

"Oh, please. We both know this is all your fault!" she snapped. "Don't insult me by pretending otherwise."

I took a few steps into the room. "My fault? What are you on?"

"I know you're the one who tipped Cromwell off about initiation," Cheyenne said, standing. "How else would he have known to conduct his ridiculous raid tonight?"

"I tipped him off? Why would I tip him off?" I asked, completely baffled.

"Obviously you found out that I had no intention of initiating your little posse of losers, so you decided to ruin the whole thing," Cheyenne blurted.

"Okay, first of all, Ms. Selective Memory," I began, "I had no idea you were planning on ostracizing them. Do you not remember how shocked I was?"

I hated to admit my naïveté, but it was the truth. And if it would get her psycho self to back off, so be it.

"So you're a good actress. Bully for you," Cheyenne said.

"Bully for me? Where do you get this stuff?" I asked.

"All I know is, a true Billings Girl would never have gone against her sisters like this," Cheyenne said, walking slowly toward me. "This is an elite house, Reed. But you don't get that, do you? You don't get that our lives are different from yours. That they will always be different. That our bonds are formed on something much deeper than you could ever hope to understand."

"On what? On money? On privilege? On Daddy's credit card?" I retorted. "Oh, yeah. That's deep."

Cheyenne sniffed, looking me up and down. "See? You've just proved it. You don't belong in our world. You have no idea what it takes to be in Billings."

She crossed her arms over her chest and her diamond *B* shifted above her neckline. That ridiculous trinket. Her superior way of separating us from the crowd. God, I wished she could have seen me in that office tonight. Someone had turned her in, yes. It was the only explanation for her expulsion. Constance? Sabine? I had no idea. But even Cromwell couldn't get away with booting her without someone's testimony. But it hadn't been mine. Oh, how I wished I could tell her it hadn't been mine.

But I knew without reservation that if the situation had been reversed, Cheyenne would have given me up without so much as a blink. I wasn't going to stand here and defend myself. I wasn't going to let her think I was begging for her approval and absolution.

"I think you're the one who has no idea what it takes," I said through my teeth.

"I hate you," Cheyenne spat, getting right in my face. "I wish you'd never come to this school. You don't belong here. You're nothing but a backwater hick, and that's all you'll ever be."

The venom dropping off her tongue seared right through me. I narrowed my eyes. "That may be true, Cheyenne, but tomorrow I'll still be an Easton Academy student. What will you be?"

Oh. My. God. I'd just said it. The perfect comeback at the perfect time. My face was hot with triumph. And an undertone of what felt, annoyingly, like guilt. But she deserved it, didn't she? After all that she'd done?

"Get out," Cheyenne said through her teeth, an angry tear spilling down her cheek. Her face was near purple with rage.

"Cheyenne—"

"Get out!"

She grabbed me, turned me around, and shoved me into the hall. Before I could even turn fully around, she'd slammed the door. I stood there for a long moment, shaking as I tried to catch my breath. I had never seen Cheyenne look like that before. It was almost frightening.

"Ms. Brennan?"

Mrs. Naylor's voice startled me half out of my skin. She stood at the end of the hall looking like grim death. A few doors in the hallway quietly closed. Clearly the girls in the house had been listening in on me and Cheyenne.

"I believe I told you all to get to bed."

"Right. Sorry," I told her, scurrying to my room.

I caught her look of disdain as I slipped inside and closed the door. Sabine sat up in her bed. The candles next to her bed were lit, and they flickered as she moved.

"Are you all right?" she asked.

I sat on my comforter, still trembling, and took a deep breath. "Fine," I replied. I swallowed hard, feeling almost nervous. "So. Interesting development."

"Yes," she replied. "Very interesting."

"Did you tell on her?" I asked.

"No," Sabine answered right away. "Did you?"

"No. But I guess we don't have to talk about that thing we weren't going to talk about."

I glanced at her quickly. She shrugged. Tried not to smile.

"I suppose not."

I slipped out of my initiation clothes, yanked a sleep shirt out of my drawer, and pulled it on. No washing up. No brushing hair. All I wanted to do right then was crawl into bed and fall into a deep sleep. My body was so exhausted, it felt ten times heavier than usual. I had a feeling that not even thoughts of Josh and Cheyenne could keep me awake tonight.

"Good night," I said to Sabine as I turned toward the wall.

"Good night."

She blew out her candles and that acrid scent of smoke filled the air. I breathed it in and sighed, trying to banish all thoughts of Cheyenne's face from my mind. She had really lost it back there. We really would all be better off with her gone.

Maybe we could finally get a little peace.

LONG GONE

I sat up straight in bed, my hand already at my heart. Someone was screaming. Screaming nonstop. I looked at Sabine. She was on her feet, her chest heaving up and down.

"What is it? What is it?" she asked.

Doors slammed. Pounding footsteps. I shoved my sheets aside. The weak sunlight was just pushing its way through the windowpanes. There was a shout. Another scream atop the first. I raced into the hall with Sabine at my heels. Vienna, on the floor against the wall, crying. London, Portia, Tiffany, and Kiki gathered at the door to Cheyenne's room. Missy and Lorna clinging to each other. Someone, somewhere, was throwing up. I got to the door, easily slipped through. Rose was still screaming. Screaming over Cheyenne's body.

"Cheyenne! Oh my God! Cheyenne!"

The voice was mine, but it seemed to be coming from somewhere outside me. I fell to my knees. Took her face in my hands. It was like clammy ice. Gray. There were tiny red dots on the skin all around her eyes.

"Cheyenne! Wake up! Cheyenne!" I shouted.

I slapped at her face with my fingers, knowing it would do nothing. Knowing it was too late.

"Stop screaming!" I roared at Rose.

Tiffany stepped forward, tiptoeing past Cheyenne as if she might catch something, and hugged Rose to her. Rose, mercifully, stopped.

"She OD'ed," London said, breathless. "She must've OD'ed."

There were pills on the floor. A small velvet bag with white pills spilling out the top. White pills with a blue-dot design on them. I felt my entire world collapse in on me. My vision grayed.

White pills with a blue-dot design . . . white pills with a blu—

Suddenly Astrid burst into the room with Mrs. Naylor. Astrid's hand flew to her mouth and she turned away from Cheyenne's body. Mrs. Naylor, more spry than I ever could have imagined, dropped down next to me and put her fingers to Cheyenne's throat. I stood up. Stood back. Gave her room.

Mrs. Naylor started CPR. Everyone was silent. Vienna's crying in the hall and the sound of Mrs. Naylor's pumping and counting were the only sounds. I looked at Tiffany. She was staring, wide-eyed, at the desk. I followed her eyes. There, sitting next to Cheyenne's pink laptop, was a piece of lavender paper. On it, written in Cheyenne's swirling script were but a few words.

I'm sorry. I can't go home.

A siren split the silence. Mrs. Naylor gave up. Sat back on her slip-pered heels. Covered her mouth with one veiny hand. We heard the paramedics slamming through the doors, into our home, but we all knew it was too late

Cheyenne was long gone.

THE MOVIE

I stood outside Billings in the warm morning sun, feeling as if I was watching a movie I had seen before. It was all so familiar. The police cars. The yellow tape. The flashing lights. Students in their pajamas, standing around, looking horrified. The crying, the wonder, the fear. The cops with their stern looks and comforting hands on shoulders. Everyone was playing their parts to perfection.

But this time there was no mist. No darkness. No dew. This time there was no uncertainty. No confusion. No accusations.

Cheyenne had killed herself. End of story. She had closed her door on me last night and sometime before Rose had opened it this morning to help her pack, she had taken her own life.

All around me people whispered and talked and speculated. All around me people stared and waited and wondered. I couldn't hear any of them. Couldn't move or focus. I could hardly even breathe.

Had she been planning it when she threw me out of her room? Was that what the out-of-control look was about? Had she already known? Already planned . . .

The front door of Billings House opened. A tall, broad EMT with a shaved head maneuvered the stretcher over the threshold. It was covered in thick white sheets, but the outline of the body was clear. Her petite frame looked tinier than ever. Cheyenne was under there. Cheyenne. Yesterday she had been laughing with Portia at lunch, studying on the quad. Today she was dead. Gone. Forever.

I saw Ivy step up out of the crowd. Stand atop one of the stone walls. Rose stepped up next to her. They stood side by side, watching silently, watching stoically as the stretcher progressed down the pathway. The doors of the ambulance opened. The legs of the stretcher collapsed. Cheyenne was loaded inside. Dead. Gone. Forever.

And suddenly, Josh appeared out of nowhere, and I was in his arms.

"Reed, omigod. Are you okay?" he demanded.

I pressed my face into his shoulder. I couldn't watch anymore. Couldn't breathe. Couldn't. Couldn't. Couldn't.

He leaned back. Took my face in both hands. Tried to look me in the eye. But I couldn't do that, either. I stared at his chest. Tiny dots swirled in front of my eyes. Prickling, pretty little dots . . .

"Reed, breathe," Josh said to me. "Breathe!"

Couldn't. Breathe. Tiny dots. There were so . . . so . . . many of them. . . .

Josh shook me hard. I sucked in air. Pain exploded in my chest. I started to cough. Doubled over. Gasping. Coughing. Not getting enough air. I was going to be sick. Sick everywhere.

"Move! Move!" I heard Josh shout. He maneuvered me over to a low stone wall that surrounded one of the gardens. I felt the coldness of the rock through my thin shorts, and it brought me back. Put my head between my knees and breathed in and out . . . in and out . . .

"It's okay. You're okay," Josh said, his hands still on my shoulders as he crouched in front of me. "Just breathe. Just breathe."

In and out. In and out. I was breathing. I could breathe. Cheyenne, however—

"Why are you being so nice to me?" I blurted, tears spilling down my cheeks.

"What?"

I lifted my head. Head rush. I gripped the stones at my sides until it passed. Blinked my eyes open. Josh's face was all concern. All innocent, desperate concern.

"Are you okay?" he asked, running his hand over my hair.

"No. No, I'm not okay. I'm so sorry, Josh!" I cried. "I didn't believe you, but it was true. It was all true."

"What was true?" he asked, placing his warm hand on my knee.

"You! The drugs. It was Cheyenne. She did it to you. I saw them. I saw the pills," I rambled. "It's what she used to . . . what she used to . . ."

And that was it. There was nothing left in me. I leaned forward onto Josh's strong shoulder and just cried. And cried and cried and cried and cried. She must have sent that text message to herself. Must have lifted his phone and set the whole thing up for me. Clearly she was desperate enough to do such a thing.

"Why would she do this? Why?" I rambled.

"It's okay, Reed," Josh whispered, holding me. He stroked my hair and whispered in my ear. "It's okay. It's going to be okay."

MORBID CURIOSITY

Sabine walked into our room later that day to find me packing my Easton soccer duffel bag. She stopped in her tracks, hand still on the doorknob.

"Where are you going?" she demanded. Almost snapped.

"Josh thought it would be a good idea to get out of here for a couple of days," I told her. "Don't worry. I'll be back."

Her entire posture relaxed. "Thank goodness. I thought you were dropping out."

"No. Not yet, anyway," I attempted to joke. Lame joke. We looked at each other and both rolled our eyes.

"Where are you going?" she asked.

She walked to her desk and sat down stiffly. All our movements had been stiff like that since that morning. As if we didn't know how to act anymore. As if that room down the hallway was somehow watching us. After the ambulance was gone and the police had done their work, only a few of the Billings Girls had come back to the house. I was sure classes would have been canceled if this were a weekday, but it was a Saturday anyway, so they were killing time in the library, on the quad, or in other dorms. The few who had returned kept their doors closed, unlike a usual day off when they would be open, music pouring into the hall, the sounds of chatter and laughter everywhere. Just thinking about it put pressure on my heart. I couldn't wait to get out of there.

"New York," I told her. "Josh's parents said it was okay if we stay at their town house. They're in France right now, so . . ."

"So you'll have the whole house to yourselves," Sabine said.

"Believe me, that's the last thing I'm thinking about right now," I replied. "I just want to get out of here."

I zipped up my bag. Looked at the door.

"I'm sorry to be leaving you right now, though," I told her. "It's kind of a bitch move, I know."

"Oh, don't worry about it," Sabine said, lifting a hand. "My sister is in Boston for a few days, so I applied for time off campus. I can't wait to see her."

"That's so nice," I said, surprised. Sabine had mentioned nothing of this before now. "I'm sorry I won't be around to meet her."

"No worries," Sabine said with a smile. "Next time. I'm sure she'd love to meet you as well." She stood up again and grabbed a book from her bag. "I think I'll go outside and find Constance and the others." Like I said, no one could stay inside Billings for long. "Have fun in the city. Try not to think about this place."

"I will," I told her, accepting a quick hug.

When she was gone, the house was as still as a tomb. I felt my pulse start to race and considered heading outside myself until it was time to go. I was about to grab my backpack and just go when my eyes fell on my computer and I paused. I hadn't checked my e-mail since yesterday morning. I wondered, with a sudden sizzle of nerves, if Dash had written. If, in the very small world we circulated in, he had already heard about what had happened. I hadn't heard from him since I'd asked if he knew how to get in touch with Noelle. But this . . . he had to have written if he'd heard about this. Tense with anticipation, I sat down and opened my browser. Sure enough, the first new e-mail was from Dash, time-stamped from late that morning. I quickly clicked it open and glanced behind me. The door was still closed.

I took a deep breath and turned back to the screen. The message was short.

> Reed,
> Don't worry. Everything happens for a reason.
> —Dash

I blinked. Read it again. Was he referring to Cheyenne, or to something that I had written to him? I couldn't imagine Dash being so cavalier about the death of someone he knew. Someone he may even have named as a friend. But what had I written to him last time that would merit that response? I found that, with everything that had happened, I couldn't even remember my wording.

I closed the message. The list reappeared. My heart completely stopped.

The second message was from Cheyenne. It was dated 2:04 that morning.

She had closed her door on me last night and sometime before Rose had opened it this morning to help her pack, she had taken her own life.

There was an e-mail in my in-box from someone who would never speak to anyone again. Never write to anyone or say another word. Why had she e-mailed me of all people? Why would she want some of her last thoughts to go to me?

My throat went dry. A sick sense of dread seeped from my shoulders all the way down through my chest and settled in my gut, writhing around like snakes inside my stomach. I felt like somebody was watching me. Watching and getting their sick, sadistic jollies from the show.

I took a deep breath. Straightened my back. Tried to look unaffected. To feel unaffected. My hand hovered over the mouse.

Just delete it. I should just delete it. Forget it was there. Pretend it never happened.

But who was I kidding? Even I was not immune to morbid curiosity. In that moment I was positive that I could not live the rest of my life in peace without knowing.

I dropped my hand. Clicked the message open. Immediately wished I hadn't. This was all it said:

Ignore the note. You did this to me. You ruined my life.

SURPRISE, SURPRISE

How did I ruin her life? How? I hadn't gotten her expelled. Hadn't named names. I should have told her. Should have told her I had protected her even after everything. Why hadn't I told her? It was just pride. My pride. Had my pride been the cause of Cheyenne's death?

"Reed?"

Josh held open the door of the glass-fronted restaurant on Perry Street. The smells emanating from inside prickled my taste buds. Too bad I was so sure my stomach was going to reject anything I tried to send its way.

"Thanks," I said as I slipped by him.

He put his hand on my arm. His fingers were so warm. "Are you okay? We don't have to eat out if you don't want to."

There had been a half-hour-long debate about whether to stay in or go out, both sides argued by Josh himself. Pro: We had just gotten back together and should celebrate. Con: How could we celebrate when someone we knew had just killed herself? I had, in my distracted state, agreed with both sides whenever they came up. Josh had been forced to finally make the decision out of hunger. I had put on my favorite blue H&M dress, not even caring if it was nice enough for wherever he was taking me, slicked my hair back into a ponytail, and followed him out of the town house.

"I'm fine," I lied. "Just hungry."

He smiled and nodded and followed me inside. The maître d' led us to a table in the center of the restaurant. The largest table in the place sat four, and the chairs were comfy, deep-winged chairs like you'd find in an upscale living room. When I sank into mine, I felt as if I were cocooned. Warm. Safe. Now if I could just concentrate on Josh all night, have an actual conversation, I might actually be able to take my mind off that e-mail.

"Oh, crap," Josh said, pausing before he could lower himself all the way into his chair.

My heart slammed into my sternum. An inordinately violent reaction. "What?"

"I see some friends of my parents," he said, lifting a hand and faking a smile. "I'm sorry, Reed, I have to go over there. Just for a minute."

My hands gripped the arms of my chair.

No. Don't leave me. Don't leave me. Don't leave me. I can't be alone right now.

"That's okay," I said, gulping.

"I promise I'll be back in two seconds," he told me.

The second he was gone, my heart started to race. Sweat prickled my underarms and down my back. She couldn't have really blamed me. She couldn't have. She had to have known that, even with all that had happened, she still had her whole life ahead of her. She could have gone to a million other private schools, would have still waltzed right into an Ivy League school. It wasn't my fault. It could not have been my—

Why is that woman staring at me like that? It's like she knows. It's like she can see right through me and—

Okay, deep breath, Reed. Cheyenne was unstable. Obviously. Even if she did blame you for her death, that means nothing. Stable people do not kill themselves. Stable people don't leave two contradicting suicide notes.

Stable people also don't have paranoid panic attacks just because their boyfriends leave the table.

It was too warm in the restaurant. The candles were sucking all the air out. I had to get out of there. Now. I fumbled for my purse. Reached for my phone. I was going to go outside and call my brother. I needed to hear a comforting voice. I needed to talk to someone I could trust.

My hands were shaking. The phone slipped from my grasp and hit the floor. An elegant hand reached down and snatched it up for me.

"Lose something, glass-licker?"

Oh. My. God.

I leaned forward, around the wings of the chair, and Noelle Lange stepped into full view. I felt as if my heart were about to burst out of my chest. It wasn't until that moment that I realized that on some level, I had believed I would never see her again.

"Noelle!"

I jumped up. Nearly knocked the heavy chair over. She stopped it with her free hand.

"Okay. Let's not get too excited," she said, rolling her eyes. "It's not like I'm back from the dead or something."

For some reason, the way she said those words, I knew that she knew about Cheyenne. And I didn't even care that she was being callous about it. All that mattered was that she was here. Miraculously, perfectly, here. I threw my arms around her and hugged her tight.

"It's so good to see you!" I said.

She hugged me back. "You too."

I looked her over as I leaned away. She looked amazing, of course. Her long brown hair shone and she'd cut long bangs that fell perfectly over her brown eyes. She wore a low-cut black wrap dress and a simple but gorgeous diamond pendant. Her colorful strappy heels were so high, she towered over me, and her bronzed legs looked toned to soccer-finals perfection.

"Where have you been?" I demanded, noting the perfect tan.

"Here and there," she said casually. "As of this week, I'm a free woman. My father's genius lawyers finally broke down La Beastesse—that's what I call the judge who was presiding over my case," she added in a conspiratorial whisper. "So my probation has officially been lifted. Whatever that means."

"What *does* that mean?" I asked.

"Basically that now I can go out of the country," she said, lifting my water glass off the table and taking a sip. "Which is *so* overdue. I could not be any more sick of the Hamptons."

"So you're . . . going out of the country?" I asked, feeling inexplicably crestfallen. It wasn't as if she was going to go back to Easton with me. Wasn't as if I could count on her living down the hall from me again. Being there for me. Protecting me.

Noelle looked me up and down. "Actually, I'm not so sure. There have been certain developments that might entice me to stay stateside."

I swallowed hard. "You don't mean . . . I mean . . . you heard about Cheyenne."

"Yes." She pursed her lips. Placed the glass down on the table. "Shame. But you know what they say, Reed."

I looked into her eyes. Those familiar, sparkling, mischievous eyes. I almost couldn't believe she was there. Couldn't believe how much I'd missed her. How much I'd missed feeling like this. Like anything could happen.

"What?" I asked. "What do they say?"

Noelle smiled knowingly. "Everything happens for a reason."